MW01138998

SOUTHERN MYTHS

SWEET TEA WITCH MYSTERIES BOOK THREE

AMY BOYLES

ONE

I stared at the egg laying on my counter. It was a deep plum jewel tone. Beautiful, really. Actually, gorgeous. If the darned egg would just stay that way, beautiful and purple and completely intact, there wouldn't be a problem.

But there was a problem.

The thing was cracking right open.

That's right. That thing was hatching as if it was dying of thirst and the creature inside knew I held a glass of the finest sweet tea.

Which I did.

I moved away from the quivering egg. "What am I supposed to do with a dragon?"

Axel Reign, aka Mr. Sexy, wove strong fingers through his dark locks. "Raise it?"

"That's not funny."

"I don't know, Pepper. I guess you're supposed to sell it to a witch for her familiar. Why else would Donovan have ordered it?"

Yes y'all, that's right. The name's Pepper Dunn and I'm a witch. Oh, and I run a sweet little pet shop in the magical town of Magnolia Cove, Alabama. The store's called Familiar Place, and I specialize in matching witches with their pet familiars.

Not all witches have familiars. I don't. A lot do, and I realize it's ironic that I am minus one furry little critter. But oh, well.

I also didn't always own this shop. My Great-Uncle Donovan left it to me several weeks ago. I'm still learning the lay of the land, and about magic. I had no idea I was related to witches—or was even a witch myself before receiving a letter and moving here. It also started a wild chain of adventures since then. Ending up with a special-delivery of a dragon's egg.

A large chunk of egg flew from the apex of the shell and landed on the linoleum floor. I gasped. Y'all, I wasn't trying to hide my fear. I was seriously nervous about a dragon.

I mean, a *dragon*.

What in tarnation was I supposed to do with a fire-breathing, treasure-stealing creature?

I shot Axel an expression filled with fear. He crossed to me and threaded his fingers through mine. "It's going to be okay."

I gripped his hand tightly. "I have a seriously hard time believing that." A fissure ripped along the side of the egg. "Why would Uncle Donovan have ordered a dragon? A dragon, Axel. It'll grow a thousand feet high. Destroy all of Magnolia Cove. Eat people. *People.*"

Axel stroked my arm. "It might be a vegetarian dragon."

I glared at him and he chuckled. "Come on. It's probably just like a dog. Could be all in how you raise it."

"Sure," I mumbled. "Whatever you say."

One of the kittens clawed her way up the side of the cage. "What is it?" she said.

"It smells funny," one of the puppies yipped.

Oh, that's right. I might've forgotten to tell you. I can communicate with animals. It's part of what makes me so good at matching witches and familiars.

It wasn't always like that. Before I inherited my witchy powers, I could barely communicate with people, much less animals.

That's not true. I can communicate with people. Sane ones anyway.

Suddenly half the egg shell blew outward, clattering across the floor. I ducked in fear, and then realized I was being ridiculous.

Axel pulled me up. "It's just a baby."

"This could be like in *Alien*," I said. "Just because it's small doesn't mean it isn't deadly."

His lips quirked in a delicious smirk—one that almost distracted me from the scary animal that might want to eat me. "You're saying you think it's deadly?"

I clutched his hand. "That's exactly what I'm saying."

He smiled as if he was holding in a laugh. "Why don't you take a look?"

I swallowed a giant knot of nerves and glanced over at the egg. A long, reptilian-like tail coiled around a small thick- skinned body. The tail slowly uncurled, revealing skin blotched in green, blue and purple. Two tiny horns erupted from both sides of the head and wide brown eyes blinked slowly at me.

It couldn't have been any larger than a two-month-old kitten, though it looked to weigh about three times as much.

The animal gazed at me, opened its mouth and grunted out a greeting that only I could understand.

"Mama," it said, staring at me.

"Um. What was that?"

"What did it say?" Axel said.

I cringed. "It called me Mama."

He laughed.

I tugged my hand from his and fisted it to my hip. "Just what exactly is so funny?"

He shook his head. "The fact that this deadly creature seems to think you're its Mama. It's like a bad Disney cartoon."

I slanted my head toward him. "And what am I supposed to do with it?"

Axel crossed to the counter, where he'd laid a sheet of paper. "It did come with instructions."

I rolled my eyes. "Does it explain how to feed it?"

Axel shook his head. "They're not that thorough."

"That doesn't help me."

I dragged my gaze to the dragon—you know, the creature that's not supposed to exist.

"Mama." Thin leather wings unfolded. The dragon leaned forward, stretching its hind legs.

Its big dark eyes continued to stare at me. The creature reminded me of a puppy dog. Its large doe-eyes were sucking me in. Beginning to make me feel responsible for it.

I wanted to extend my hand, but the thing looked scaly and it was also kind of wet from being in the egg. I pressed my lips together and stepped forward. Lifting my hand, I attempted to bring it to the creature, but I was not a reptile person. So as much as I wanted to offer some comfort, I just couldn't bring myself to do it.

"Mama," it said.

Axel swooped in. "Come here, little guy."

"Are you sure it's a boy?"

"Most definitely. I got a good look when it stretched."

He grabbed a clean rag that I kept for wiping surfaces and dried the baby. "There you go. Is that better?"

Axel rubbed behind its ear and the dragon closed its eyes as if enjoying the scratch. Its tongue lolled to one side and I felt a smile light my face.

He picked up the creature and hugged it to his chest. The wings wrapped around Axel and the creature said, "Mama."

I giggled.

Axel's blue eyes flared with confusion as he glanced at me. "What is it?"

"He thinks you're his Mama now."

Axel frowned. "Definitely not. Here. You want to hold him?"

I shrank away. "Really. I don't know. It's not my thing, you know, touching reptiles and cuddling with them."

"It's a dragon. How many times in your life are you going to be able to say you hugged one?"

"Well, one. Right now."

He rolled his eyes. "It was sent to your shop. Just hug it."

I shook my head and sighed. "Fine. But then I'm calling the place that sent it and returning it. I don't need a dragon."

Axel pulled the creature from his chest and brought it over to me, pressing its cold, wet nose into my shoulder.

"What. Are. You. Doing?"

Axel grinned. "Letting this little guy get a good whiff of his mom."

"Sorry?"

He heaved the dragon toward my chest. I cringed. Axel scowled. "He needs to smell you. Learn your scent so that he knows who's taking care of him."

I shook my head. "That's not me."

"You're the one who speaks to animals," Axel said.

I shrugged. "So?"

"Will you just take him?"

Axel pushed him to my chest and let go. My arms shot instinctively around the dragon and I clutched him to me. Big weepy eyes stared up at me and my heart broke a little for the reptile. Or mythological creature.

"It may need to eat," Axel prodded.

I glared at him. "Would you like to feed it? Maybe it likes dog food."

Axel shook his head. "My guess is he wants something fresh—like a mouse you feed the snakes. But I'll try kibble while you call the sender."

I held the dragon close while I riffled through the papers that came with him. I found the invoice with a phone number and dialed.

A gruff man with a thick New York accent answered. "Magical Creatures," he said in a nasal voice.

"Um. Hello. My name is Pepper Dunn and I own Familiar Place."

"You must be from down South," he said.

I cleared my throat. "Yes, I am. We are. The shop's in Magnolia Cove, Alabama."

"Alabama," he exclaimed. "That explains it. What can I do for you, dear?"

"Listen, I just received a dragon's egg in the mail."

"Let me see...hold on." I could hear papers shuffling in the background. "That's right. We got an order for a dragon egg about two months ago from one Donovan Craple."

"Yes. It's arrived. Thing is, I don't need a dragon. Can I return it?"

The man laughed. "Lady, if I had a nickel for everyone who said they didn't need a dragon, I'd only have one nickel. Everybody wants a dragon. And trust me, Donovan Craple paid top dollar for that dragon. There are no refunds, no returns, no exchanges on live creatures. I'm afraid you're stuck with it."

"Great," I said.

"But if you need help, there's lots of information on our website about caring for dragons. When they first hatch, they're hungry. The best thing to do is feed them a small mouse."

Awesome. I owned a carnivorous beast that would probably eat me as it grew. "I'll be sure to check the website."

I hung up as Axel entered with a bowl of dog food. "How'd it go?" he said.

I shook my head. "Not well. It turns out we're stuck with this guy."

Axel set the bowl on the counter. I picked up a square of food and placed it in front of the dragon. The little guy sniffed and glanced at me as if asking what he was supposed to do with it.

"Mama," he said.

I sighed. "I think you were right. We'll have to give him a mouse. Which you can do all alone," I said. "I'm not interested in watching."

Axel laughed. "Okay. But it's not my dragon."

An idea hit me. "Do you think Donovan ordered this for someone?"

Axel cocked his head. "Probably."

"So you think there might be a record of it in his office?"

Axel nodded. "Probably."

"Great. I'll start looking."

Just then, the shop door blew open as if a great gust of wind had pushed it from the heavens. A tall, slender man wearing a black cape strode in. A large emerald clasped at his throat cinched the cape together.

"I am the great Mysterio," he announced. "I'm in town to show off my magical wonders. I have heard much of this store, Familiar Place, and am in search of my pet mate."

Pet mate? I'd heard familiars called lots of things—well, not really *lots*. But I'd never heard them called mates.

I gave him a warm smile and said, "I'd be happy to help you. We've got cats, dogs, birds."

With a flourish of his cape, Mysterio pretty much answered. "I do not want some run of the mill animal. I, the great Mysterio require something much more rare and exotic than that."

His gaze flashed around the shop until it landed on the dragon.

His voice rose about three octaves. "Is that a dragon?"

"It is."

Mysterio drummed his fingers together as if plotting his next magic trick, or whatever it was he was going to do in town.

He charged over to the counter. Drool practically dripped from his mouth when he spoke. "That's it! That's the most exotic of creatures that I've been searching for. My entire life I've wanted a dragon, but they're incredibly difficult to find, much less to grow to adulthood. Is it for sale?"

I glanced at the doe-eyes and sweet little face of the guy who called me "Mama". My heart jumped a little at the thought of selling him. I glanced at Axel, who shook his head.

"Think about this Pepper. You don't know why Donovan ordered the dragon."

I scratched my lip. "I don't need this thing scaring off customers. Since I didn't order it, I don't think it's my responsibility."

Axel grazed his knuckles over his jaw. "It's a mythological creature and it's in your shop."

Mysterio wiggled his eyebrows. "I will take the greatest care of this animal. You can trust me."

Axel scowled.

I touched his arm. "Is there something you're not telling me?"

Axel opened his mouth. Shut it. "Do what you want. But I think you should wait on selling."

He stared at Mysterio as if he were trying to figure out exactly how much pig dung the guy was full of. My guess was one hundred percent.

Mysterio seemed like a swindler, a goofball and someone completely out of touch with reality.

Call it the cape and the fact that he was in a witch town about to perform a magic show, or whatever.

Even given all that, I glanced at the dragon.

Mysterio braced his hands on the counter. "I'll pay whatever you want for it."

I inhaled a deep shot of air and said, "Sold."

TWO

"*Y*ou sold a dragon? Why?" Betty Craple, my grandmother and resident sourpuss, said when I arrived home later that afternoon.

I hooked my purse on a peg and shrugged. "Apparently Uncle Donovan had ordered one before he died. It came in today and to be honest, I didn't want anything to do with the creature."

Betty tapped a wooden spoon on the cauldron nestled above a crackling fire in the hearth. She closed one nostril and the spoon zipped up to a peg and hooked itself above the mantel. "Did you ever stop to think that maybe Donovan had ordered the dragon for someone?"

I nodded. "I did. But I didn't have a chance to search his records before a buyer showed up."

Betty tugged at her silver curls. The wig she wore slid in one direction. "And you think that gives you the right to sell a dragon?"

The door opened and my cousins, Amelia and Cordelia entered. Betty turned to them, glaring. "Pepper sold a dragon today."

Amelia's eyes widened. "Oh, that is so cool. That fact that you had one. And the fact that you sold one. Why didn't you call me? I've always wanted to see a dragon. They breathe fire, you know."

9

Cordelia wrapped a hand on Amelia's shoulder. "Breathe. Just breathe."

Amelia laughed nervously. "I know, it's just I've never seen one."

Cordelia cocked her head to one side. Her long blond hair fell in her face. "And now you've gone and shattered all her hopes and dreams."

I shook my head. "I figured y'all would've seen a dragon before."

Cordelia dropped her purse on the floor and said, "We might live in a magical town, but there's tons we don't know about."

"Like dragons," Amelia said. "Who'd you sell it to?"

Betty grabbed the spoon and rapped it on the cast iron cauldron. "Doesn't matter who she sold it to. We need to get it back."

I crossed to the table where I poured myself a glass of sweet tea from the pitcher resting on it. "No way am I asking for it back. Do none of y'all realize that dragons are dangerous? I've seen all *The Hobbit* movies. That Smog guy—"

"Smaug," Cordelia corrected.

"Whatever. That is one dangerous creature. I don't think my liability insurance would cover it if the thing burned this town to matchsticks. Anyone bother to think about that?"

Amelia clicked her tongue. "You've got a good point."

I picked up a carrot stick sitting on the table and started crunching. "That's what I'm saying. I'm trying to be responsible here, make sure no one gets killed."

"So you sold it," Betty said sourly. "Did you ever happen to think that Donovan ordered it for *you*?"

I laughed because that was the most asinine thing I'd ever heard in like my entire life. "Heck no, I didn't think that. Donovan was alive when he ordered it. He wasn't sick, and that's the only reason why I ended up with the key to Familiar Place—because he sent it when he was sick. According to Magical Creatures, Donovan ordered the dragon two months ago."

"For your information," Betty said, jerking her head left and right, "when a witch becomes the person who matches familiars with their owners, they receive their own familiar."

I sank into a chair. "I don't have one. You didn't get me one."

Betty snapped some dried herbs from a stick above the fireplace. She ground them in her palms and sprinkled it into the cauldron.

"It would've been Donovan's responsibility to do that since you were next in line to receive the shop."

I shook my head. "But a familiar can't be bought for a witch. They have to be matched."

Betty's eyes sparkled as she said, "Exactly. Your uncle may've known more about you than you think."

I shook my head. "I'm not buying it."

"Well, you'd better be pulling your wallet from your purse, because you need to get that dragon back. I believe Donovan bought it for you."

"No."

She rubbed her chin. "Who'd you sell it to, anyway?"

I yawned. "Some Mysterio guy. He's in town doing a magic show or something."

My cousins exchanged a look with Betty.

"What?" I said.

"Mysterio's a hoax," Amelia said. "He travels through towns telling little old ladies that he can communicate with their loved ones—dead children, spouses. You name it, and if it's deceased, Mysterio claims he can speak to it."

"He comes every year," Cordelia said. "We haven't gone to his performance in ages. Though for a wizard, he puts on a great show for witches. There are all kinds of ghosts and whatnot."

I frowned. "So does he really speak to people's dead loved ones?"

"What do you think?" Betty snapped.

I shrugged. "No clue. You tell me."

"For regular folks what Mysterio does is all hocus-pocus—smoke and mirrors. But for us, it's the real deal—it has to be since we're witches. Oh, ghosts appear all right, but the ghosts are charlatans, pretending to be other folks' loved ones."

I rubbed my forehead, trying to stop the headache threatening to bloom from all this confusion. "So the ghosts are real but pretending to be someone else?"

"Right," Cordelia said. "Still, the witches who want to communicate with the dead are so distraught they generally don't realize they're being taken advantage of."

"Wow," I said, "this Mysterio guy sounds like a horrible person."

"Charlatan," Cordelia said.

Betty fixed her wig and hiked her old lady jeans up until the waistband rested just under her boobs. "And that charlatan now has a baby dragon." She pointed an accusatory finger at me. "A dragon that rightfully belongs to you."

A whirlwind of anxiety knotted my stomach. I raked my fingers through my hair, afraid of what would happen next. "So what are we going to do? Let Mysterio keep it?"

Betty shook her head. "Nope. You and me, kid, we're going to get it back. If Donovan wanted you to have it, it was for a good reason." She glanced at Cordelia and Amelia. "Get dressed, girls. We've got a show to attend."

THREE

J had time to eat a light dinner of country-fried steak, mashed potatoes and fried okra. They were all small portions, so that's what I call light. Then I showered and changed into a little black dress before showtime.

"Where are y'all off to?" Mattie asked.

Mattie was a gray cat that had belonged to my mother when she lived in Betty's house. Mattie's general residence was the window seat in my bedroom, but today she lazed on the bed.

"We're going to see this guy Mysterio. Do you know him?"

Mattie yawned. "'Course I know him, sugarbear. That man's been swindling folks since I was a kitten."

I ran a brush through my hair. "I don't understand why people let him. Seems to me that he would've been run out of town ages ago."

Mattie shook her head. "There's always someone who believes in Mysterio, and that someone in this town is Idie Claire Hawker."

My jaw dropped. "Idie Claire? You mean the town gossip?"

"One and the same. She might not strike you as such, but Idie Claire's got enough pull in this town that if she wanted to up and move it, that would happen."

I stared at Mattie. "Idie Claire. We're talking about the same woman, right?"

Mattie rubbed her paw over her whiskers. "Same one. Only one. Now sugar, you best be gettin' along if you're going to watch the show. Starts at eight pm sharp. Most of the town'll be there. Folks always love to see what Mysterio cooks up for 'em."

I slipped on a pair of heels. "All right, and thanks for the head's up."

I zipped downstairs, where the rest of my family waited for me. Betty was handing out small canisters that looked like pepper spray. She pressed the warm steel into my palm.

"What's this?"

"It's a spray that'll keep you from getting caught up in Mysterio's antics. It'll help you keep a cool head."

I glanced at the sleek black lacquered coating. "Why do I need my own? Can't you just spray me and we go?"

Betty pulled her corncob pipe from a pocket and shoved it in her mouth. "Sometimes y'all need extra. Mysterio has a strange effect on women."

"He's old," I said. "At least fifty."

"You youngsters," Betty said. "A fifty-year-old man chasing me would be a dream come true."

Cordelia smacked her lips. "Maybe we can help you achieve that dream."

Betty snarled at her. "Watch it. When I need one of y'all to help me find a man, I'll let you know."

We walked from the house to Bubbling Cauldron Road, where most of downtown sat. The town theater, aptly named *The Magnolia*, was crowded. Folks jammed the sidewalk. Could I blame them? Mysterio only came around once a year. You had to see him when you could. After all, how often did folks get to see ghosts live in the flesh?

Okay, so maybe they weren't exactly in the flesh, but I think you get the picture.

The line moved quickly and Betty was able to snag tickets front and center. "How'd you do that?" I said.

"I told the house manager I'd wither certain body parts if he didn't give us the best."

Amelia leaned over. "Ew. You threatened him?"

Betty rolled her eyes. "I never said *whose* body parts would get shriveled."

"Very saucy of you," I said.

The lights blackened. "Shh. Watch the show." Then she dug something out of her purse and squirted me.

"Uh. That's cold and now I'm all wet."

Betty winked at me as she shook the canister. "Better wet than taken."

"What? Is this a Liam Neeson movie?" I said.

Amelia flared out her arms. "Is he going to show up? He can take me anywhere."

"He's old enough to be your father," Betty said.

Amelia fluffed the tips of her pixie haircut. "I'd erase my age limit on men for him."

Betty grinned. "Really? I'll remember that."

Amelia rolled her eyes. "Don't think about fixing me up with a Liam Neeson lookalike. Last time you tried to match me, it turned out horrible."

"Shh," Cordelia said. "It's starting."

The house had gone black. Low lights glowed onstage. A flash of lightning cracked on a platform and Mysterio appeared, arms outstretched. His voice boomed when he spoke. A shiver raced along my spine as he commanded the theatergoers to submit to him.

"Welcome, ladies and gentlemen. For those of you who do not know me, I am the great Mysterio. *Tonight*," he punched the word, "I will connect you to your loved ones. Tonight you will be dazzled by the otherworld, amazed at who you will see again. You will be left without wondering, without fearing about what happened to your loved ones when they crossed over. For tonight, you will have answers. So now, let's start the show!"

A cloud of smoke erupted where he stood. The audience exploded into applause. When the smoke cleared, Mysterio appeared at the foot of the stage with his hands cupped in front of him and his eyes closed.

"A John is coming through. Does someone know a John?"

"Only half the people here," Cordelia whispered in my ear.

I smirked. No doubt that was true.

A hand shot up. "I do. I know a John."

I leaned forward. The hand belonged to Idie Claire. Boy, my family wasn't kidding when they said she loved this whole ghost thing.

"And John," Mysterio said, his voice wavering, "John was your…"

"Father," Idie said.

Mysterio pressed his fingers to his temples. "He died from harsh circumstances."

"In bed. It was the end of his life," Idie said.

Okay, so maybe not harsh circumstances, but he did die.

"John wants to come through," Mysterio said.

Behind him, a figure appeared from wisps of smoke. There stood a man wearing a plaid shirt, a wide-brimmed farmer's hat and black boots.

"Daddy never farmed," Idie said.

I bit back a laugh.

"This is how the spirit looks," Mysterio explained. "Your daddy said he felt this way on the inside, even though he lived a different sort of life."

Betty rolled her eyes wide for me to see.

"Okay," Idie said quietly.

"He says there's something important that's hiding behind a portrait."

"What?" Idie said. "We don't have a portrait."

Amelia giggled.

Mysterio cleared his throat. "That's what he said. But maybe he didn't mean portrait. Maybe he meant…toilet?"

Idie pressed a finger to her lips in thought. "Maybe so. Maybe that's what he meant."

The ghostly figure pointed toward the door as if he needed Idie to hurry up and find whatever was hidden behind the toilet.

I tried not to laugh.

"That's all John has to say," Mysterio said. He waved a hand and the apparition vanished.

"Another voice is coming through. Another voice—this one is harder to focus on. I hear the name Salt. Does anyone know a Salt?"

No one said anything. Mysterio cleared his throat. "Wait. That was a nickname. The real one is coming. Sassafras. Does anyone have a loved one by that name?"

My throat dried. My mother. Sassafras had been my mother. I shot a confused look to Betty, whose eyes were about the size of buckeyes and ready to pop right out of her head.

I slowly raised my hand. "I know a Sassafras."

Mysterio smiled at me. "Come to us, Sassafras. Come let us see you and you see us."

A plume of smoke rose up behind him. The wisps coiled and tightened, hardening until a figure appeared. A woman with long flowing hair bobbed above the stage. Her hair and dress floated as if she were submerged underwater. Her eyes were completely white, the irises missing and her mouth quirked into a secretive smile.

I gasped. So did Cordelia and Amelia.

"Aunt Saltie," Amelia whispered.

"Mom," I whimpered.

The ghost stared out into the audience. She didn't move, didn't interact. I wanted her to look in my direction, to find me.

I started to stand. Betty grabbed my hand as if warning me not to, but I couldn't help myself. This was my mom. The woman who died giving birth to me. I wanted to look her in the face—even if it was a ghostly one.

The figure turned in my direction. I felt the eyes light on me. A flood of emotion rushed through my body and I became dizzy.

"This woman was important to you," Mysterio said.

My voice squeaked. "Yes. Yes."

Mysterio moved his hands as if leading an invisible orchestra. "She wants you to know that she loves you. Very much. She also wants you to know you're on the right path, doing the right things."

"Does she…does she visit me often?"

The figure floated wordlessly as Mysterio wiggled his fingers toward his temples—he looked as if he was receiving transmissions from outer space.

"She's with you more than you know. Our link is fading. Sassafras is leaving us."

I reached out. "No. Don't leave."

The crowd gasped. Like it was some major faux-pas to admit I didn't want a loved one to leave. I didn't care. This was the closest I'd ever been to my mother. Yes, I realized she was dead, but this was still something to me—a shimmering ray of light that I could grasp onto and hold, if only for a moment.

Mysterio's voice boomed. "There's something she wants you to know—but she's asked me to share it with you after the show."

The ghostly figure of my mother reached out as her image faded to black. Hot tears trickled down my face. I palmed them away. When I sat, Betty plucked several tissues from a packet in her purse and handed them to me.

"He must've known you were coming," she said.

I squinted at her. "You don't think that was Mom?"

Betty's lower lip tightened. "I've never seen Mysterio conjure a true relative. All the others seem to be fake. Take Idie's. You think that was her dad?"

I shrugged as I wedged into the seat. I didn't know if that was Idie's father. It's not as if I'd met him before he died.

But the image of my own mother had been real. That was her. It looked exactly like every picture I'd never seen. But Betty was clutching strong to the fact that Mysterio was a charlatan.

Yet if that hadn't been my mother, who was it?

I WATCHED the rest of the show in silence, thinking the whole time about Mom and how I wanted to talk to Mysterio more, see what it was she had wanted to share privately with me.

"Probably the treasure map to my jewels," Betty said. "I don't trust that man."

The show was over; the house lights had come on. Most of the folks in town were heading toward the door.

They were moving slowly, but one woman with long dark hair and wearing bright red lipstick nearly knocked me over to reach the exit.

"Oh, I'm so sorry," she said.

I instantly recognized her. "Gretchen Gargoyle," I said.

She brushed her long hair from her shoulder and squinted at me. "Do I know you?"

I grimaced. "Yeah. My aunts brought me to your store, Witch's Wardrobe, a few days ago."

Gretchen's face hardened. "That's right. You destroyed my shop."

I twisted my fingers nervously. "I'm sorry about that."

She eyed me up and down. "Sure."

The dress designer strode away and I felt like a Grade A idiot for about half a second, until Betty hooked her hand around my elbow.

"You'd better get a move on, kid."

I agreed. "Yeah, I want to know about that message from Mom."

"That line of hooey? That's a crock. You don't need to worry about it. You need to get that dragon."

I rolled my eyes. "Not this again. Okay, I'll get the stupid dragon, but I don't see why I should. I don't want to be liable for the animal."

Betty pressed her lips together so hard her chin nearly touched her nose. "You don't see the importance of it? Kid, by ordering that dragon, your uncle may've saved your life."

We reached the lobby, where we followed a slowly trickling line of people. "What are you talking about?"

"If you pair with that dragon, what do you think it would be good for?"

"Burning down villages and stealing treasure?"

Betty thumped my head.

"Ouch."

"Use your brains. What else can a dragon do?"

I shook my head in frustration. "I don't know."

19

"Protection. That dragon can offer you protection."

I lifted my palms, still not understanding. "From what?"

Betty shouldered her handbag. "From *whom*, not from what. Who's the one person you've been trying to avoid since you got here."

The blood rushed to my feet as I suddenly realized what she was talking about. The mysterious Rufus had attacked me before I came to Magnolia Cove. He'd also attacked me a few days ago, when he'd been allowed into town for his mother's funeral. He'd said that since I was a head witch, he wanted my mind.

I stopped, forcing Betty to pause. "You're saying..." My voice faltered.

Betty nodded. "I'm saying that dragon can protect you from Rufus."

I cleared my throat. "Well, then what the heck are we waiting for? Let's go get it."

FOUR

I waited outside Mysterio's dressing room, behind a long line of folks. It was several minutes before I had a chance to speak with him. The place was pretty lavish. Persian rugs covered the floor, framed posters of past presenters draped the walls and low watt lamps were sprinkled around, giving the place a warm glow.

Mysterio pulled on a black turban with a feather sticking from it. "You're here about the ghost who had more to tell?"

I grimaced. "Yes, I am, but I also came to tell you I made a mistake. I never should've sold you the dragon. See, it was a gift to me. I didn't know that at the time, but I do now. Is it okay if I take it back?"

Mysterio gestured. A large birdcage floated up to us. Mysterio yanked off a silky purple covering. The little dragon lay curled up on a bed of straw. When it saw me, it yawned and blinked.

"Mama."

Wow. Now I really felt bad for letting it go.

Mysterio ran a thumb along the side of the cage. "You may not have it. You sold it fair and square. Do you realize how rare a dragon is?"

I toed the floor in embarrassment. "Yes, well I do. But here's the thing—I need the dragon for myself."

Mysterio eyed me. He leaned forward and gave me a smile that sent a shudder ripping along my spine. "Maybe we can come to an understanding." He wiggled his brows as his gaze swept over me, giving me the heebie-jeebies.

Ew. Was this guy insinuating what I think he was insinuating?

I was so not interested in that sort of agreement.

Not even to win back a dragon.

I cleared my throat. "Okay. Um. Well…what was it my mother wanted to tell me? What couldn't she say in public?"

The door opened and Gretchen Gargoyle, the women I'd ticked off in her shop, entered. When she saw me her eyes narrowed to slitty wedges of death.

"Mysterio, we're going to be late," she said.

He took my hand and said, "I must be off, but I will tell you what she said soon." I felt him wedge a slip of paper into my palm. He turned toward Gretchen. "Darling, let's be off."

With that, Mysterio left me alone in the room to wonder what it was my mother had wanted me to know.

I glanced at the dragon. My fingers itched to take him, to grab him. I licked my lips, trying to figure out if I could get away with stealing him.

Wow. Where had my morals gone?

Of course, I'd leave a check for him, so it's not like I'd just take the creature.

But still. That might cause problems. Deciding I'd find another way to get the dragon, I turned to go.

"Mama," it said.

I closed my eyes. The door opened and Betty waddled through. "Great. You got the dragon. Let's get out of here."

I shook my head. "He won't sell it. Though I'm pretty sure he'll accept sexual favors if I'm willing to offer them."

"No good Southern granddaughter of mine's going to give away her body. You're too young. Now someone like me?"

I rubbed my head. "Don't go there."

"I'm not," Betty said, pushing up her sleeves. "What I was going to say is—someone like me might do a little influencing, get him to hand the dragon over. In fact, I might be able to get Mysterio to think the whole thing was his idea."

I frowned. "How?"

Betty clapped her hands. When she opened them, the canister filled with protection liquid appeared in her palm. She spritzed some on the cage.

"I thought that was for us."

"On humans, it works to keep your head screwed on straight. But on animals, it works differently."

"How?"

"Mysterio will start to think that this sweet little dragon isn't as sweet as he originally thought."

I tipped my head. "What do you mean?"

"The spray will make the dragon appear evil, mean. By this time tomorrow, Mysterio will be begging you to take the dragon from him." Betty smiled widely. "Just you wait and see."

She turned to leave. I followed behind and unfolded the slip of paper Mysterio had given me. It listed an address, room number and time—tomorrow at eight pm. Hopefully, by then I'd know two things: the first was what my mother had wanted to tell me and the second was how much getting the dragon back would cost.

I SPENT the next day keeping myself busy at work. I cracked my knuckles to the point they wouldn't crack anymore, which was saying a lot.

Basically, I stared at the clock all day, willing it to be eight so that I could meet up with Mysterio.

"Hey there," came a gruff voice.

I glanced up to see Axel standing in the doorway. I'd been so consumed with my thoughts I hadn't heard him enter.

"Hey, yourself."

He leaned a hip against a counter, crossed his arms and gazed at me with such a deep look my knees jellied. "So did you go see Mysterio last night?"

I tucked loose strands of crimson and honey hair behind an ear. "I did. How'd you know?"

He smiled. "Half the town went."

"But not you."

He shook his head. "That man's not going to tell me anything I don't already know."

I shrugged. "You don't know until you know."

"But you also don't know what you don't know until you don't know it."

"Stop trying to outdo me."

Axel chuckled. "Done. So. Want to grab dinner tonight? I know this great little nook that serves the best fried chicken around."

"Oh? We going to Betty's house?"

He laughed again. "No."

I shot him a teasing smile. Axel placed a hand on the counter, effectively blocking my path. Musk and pine trickled from his shirt to my nose.

"I'd love to eat fried chicken but only if you come with me to meet Mysterio. I need to get back my dragon."

He rolled his eyes. "Now you've decided you need it?"

"It might help fight off Rufus."

He jumped on the counter and sat. "Done."

A flicker caught my eye. I peered around Axel and saw Mysterio walking down the street. A leggy blonde had her arm wrapped around his.

"Boy this guy gets around," I said.

Axel hopped off the counter and came around. He placed a hand on my shoulder. "Mysterio? Guy's got a girl in every town."

"Or two," I said. "I saw him with Gretchen Gargoyle last night." I motioned to the couple. "Who's the blonde?"

Axel frowned. "Why're you asking me?"

"Because you're the only private detective I know in town."

He nodded. "Good point. The blonde is Hattie Hollypop. She owns the jewelry store—Brews and Jewels."

"Brews and Jewels?"

"They also serve beer," he said.

I laughed. "Original."

Axel held my gaze and I started to feel the tension rise around us. It was like a cloud of electric pressure building and thickening. I tried to breathe, but I was mesmerized by Axel's glance.

I waited as his head dipped toward me.

The bell above the door tinkled. I jerked and found Betty Craple striding in. "I was walking past and saw you two about to kiss."

I practically jumped as far from Axel as I could get. "So you figured you'd ruin the moment."

"Right," she said proudly.

Axel dragged his gaze from Betty to me. "See you tonight."

I waved as he left. As soon as he disappeared down the street, Betty straightened her wig. "Now that my work here is done, I'll be going."

"Thanks," I said. "See you at the house."

I got home late afternoon. Betty had dinner on the table, but I did my best to ignore the scents of turnip greens, butter beans, cornbread and country ham. Saliva nearly poured from my mouth as I gazed at the spread.

"Come on and chow down," Betty said. "Your cousins should be home soon."

I shook my head. "No thanks. I've got dinner plans."

She grabbed a skillet from the fireplace and laid it on the table. "Suit yourself, but you're missing one fine meal."

"I know."

The door banged open and Cordelia stomped in. Her long hair was plastered to her forehead. She dumped her purse on the floor and sank into a chair.

"You look beat," I said.

Cordelia slicked her matted tresses. "I am. Everything was going fine at the inn and then suddenly we all had to rush around."

"Why?" I said.

"Mysterio decided to check out. And he always brings tons of luggage and requires extra care."

I stopped. "Wait. Mysterio's leaving? Why's he leaving? He can't leave."

Cordelia shrugged. "He is. Right now."

I threw Betty a panicked look. "But he's got the dragon and the message from my mom. He can't go."

Cordelia crossed one leg over the other and yanked off her shoe. "Well, if you want to catch him you'd better hurry, 'cause like I said, he's checking out."

In a flicker, all my expectations were dashed. The message from my mother—gone. The thing that could protect me from Rufus—also gone. Mysterio the mysterious, who had walked into my life yesterday was now about to leave with the knowledge I desperately needed.

I glanced at Betty. "You ready to get Mysterio?"

She winked at me. "Let's roll."

FIVE

*W*e reached the inn about five minutes later. Had to love Magnolia Cove. Most places were moments away from most other places. The town was so small, if you threw a chicken leg, you were liable to either hit a person or a building.

That's a good old-fashioned Southern witticism for you.

Betty had pulled on her running shoes. She wore white nurse-type tights and a floral print dress. She clipped along at a pretty good rate, keeping pace with me.

"Where do you think he is?" I said, inhaling a deep breath. "If Mysterio's still here."

Betty sniffed the air. She cocked one eye toward the rear of the parking lot. "I caught a whiff of cheap cologne and lipstick coming from the Dumpsters."

"Lipstick?"

She laid a beady eye of superiority on me. "Kissing," she said, as if that explained it all.

In a way, I guess it did.

We raced to the rear, where I saw Mysterio inspecting his vehicle's tires. A van with a giant bobbing black hat on top and the words

EXPERIENCE THE MYSTERIOUS scribbled on the side idled quietly.

Mysterio saw us. He backed away. "Here, you can take this thing," he said. He yanked open the van door and thrust his hands inside. When they reappeared, Mysterio was holding a gilded cage. The baby dragon opened its mouth. A spark lit and a small stream of fire erupted from its throat before petering into smoke.

I leaned over and shot Betty an I-told-you-so look. What did I say about the creature?

Dangerous.

Mysterio shoved the cage in my arms. "It's trying to kill me. Take it. You can have it. I don't want the thing. I've got to get out of here before it kills me."

I handed the cage to Betty, who immediately started cooing at the dragon. Not kidding. She sounded like a new mother soothing a baby to sleep.

Mysterio hopped in the driver's side. The black hat atop the van teetered on a loose spring.

I grabbed hold of his arm through the open window. "Wait. I need you to tell me what my mother said. What she told you last night. I have to know."

Mysterio threw the side of his cape over one shoulder. "Your mother?"

"Yes," I said. "Sassafras."

His face lighted as if he suddenly remembered. "Yes." His lips curved into a slow winding smile that made my stomach lurch. "Yes, I wrote it on a sheet of paper."

Hope zinged through my body. He hadn't left and whatever my mother wanted to me to know was somewhere.

"Where?" I said.

He opened his mouth to answer and I leaned in, a thousand cells of anticipation floating through my body. Without warning, the cape draped over his shoulders suddenly wrapped itself around Mysterio and started to smother him.

"Help," he yelled.

I grabbed hold of the fabric, trying to rip it away, but it held fast. I glanced at Betty. "What can you do?"

Betty placed a thumb over her nostril and exhaled. A snort of sparkles shot through the air, landing on the cloak.

I yanked, but the fabric squeezed him tight.

"It's not helping," I said.

Betty put the cage down and rubbed her hands together. A shower of magical streamers flew through the air onto Mysterio. Inside the cape, I could hear him gasping for air.

I pulled again, but the cape didn't loosen.

"It's not working."

I tugged the door open and Mysterio slumped to the asphalt. He kicked and bucked as I yanked, trying to pry him loose. Pain ripped up my hand as fingernails broke.

"Help," I yelled.

"Help," Betty yelled.

I buried my fingers deep in the fabric and used my body weight to tear the cape away. The fabric gave, and I skidded across the ground.

My rear end burned. I rose and rubbed it.

"You ripped a hole in your jeans," Betty said.

"Nothing a little magic can't fix," I said. I slowly made my way over to Mysterio, hoping to find him gasping for breath.

Instead, I glanced onto blue skin and sightless, glazed eyes.

"Well, looks like Mysterio bit the dust," Betty said. "Death by cape. Not pretty at all."

"No, it's not," I said. "But how? What happened?"

"Someone killed him," came a voice from behind.

I glanced over my shoulder and saw the new sheriff in town—Garrick Young. He was a tall drink of water with dark brown hair and eyes. He pinched two fingers over the rim of his hat and slid them down.

"How do you know someone killed him?" I said, rising.

Garrick looked me up and down. "Because folks don't commit suicide using their capes to kill them." His dark gaze hit me hard, sending a spear of anxiety straight to my core. "And standing over his body I find the two of you. The same two ladies I found standing over a body only about a week ago."

I cringed. "Are you saying this doesn't look good?"

Garrick dipped his head and stared at me out from under the rim of his hat. "I'm saying it doesn't look good at all."

SIX

*B*etty sat next to me at the station. The caged baby dragon rested on her lap while I twiddled my thumbs, waiting for a Christmas miracle to save us because this did not look good.

At all.

I wondered if crossing my fingers would make a Christmas miracle come sooner rather than later.

"We're going to need a miracle," Betty said.

"I was just thinking that."

She leaned over. "But at least you got the dragon."

I rested my head on the wall. "I guess your potion worked."

She sniffed. "You guess?"

"Okay. Your potion worked. That animal breathes fire and it isn't even housebroken."

She patted my hand. "Don't worry. I know the best dragon tamer in these parts."

I cocked a brow at that. "You do? Who?"

"Name's Barry."

I barked out a laugh so hard tears stung my eyes. I choked as I tried to calm myself.

Betty eyed me disdainfully. In other words, her expression twisted as if the worst smell in the world had settled in front of her face. "I take it you don't approve of his name."

I knuckled a fresh tear from my eyelash. "I'm sorry but Barry the Dragon Tamer is not who I'd expect to help me with this little guy."

Betty sniffed. "Not everyone can be named Fabio."

I broke out into another set of giggles. When I finally got hold of myself, I shook my head. "Fabio's not a good name, either."

"What name does sound good for a dragon tamer?"

I scratched my chin. "Um…Axel?"

"You're biased."

"I suppose so."

A door opened and Garrick stuck his head out. He motioned for us to come inside. Betty walked in front of me, still holding the cage.

We entered the office. Stacks of papers rimmed Garrick's desk, and numerous glass awards sat on the shelves behind him.

"Did you see anyone with Mysterio?" he said after we'd sat.

I shook my head. "No one."

He glanced at Betty. "As the girl said."

"Did he say if he'd talked to anyone?"

"No," I said. "He was in a hurry to leave, but he didn't say it was because of any one person. But I mean, heck, it's a town full of witches. Everyone can do magic. They might've evaporated right before we showed up."

Betty cocked an eye at me. "Evaporated?"

I winked at her. "Yep. Went poof."

Garrick scraped his fingers down his face. "And where'd the dragon come from?"

Betty's pouched out her lips defiantly. "This here creature belongs to Pepper fair and square. Her Uncle Donovan ordered it for her. She sold it to Mysterio before she realized the importance of the creature, but Mysterio returned it."

"Right before he died," I added. "He handed the dragon over. We didn't steal it. I don't steal. I really don't believe in it. I might've thought about stealing the dragon when Mysterio wouldn't originally return it to me, but I didn't because I'm a good Southern gal and my dad raised me right. So that means I don't steal. No sir."

Garrick stared at me for about five beats before his jaw dropped and a glazed look of confusion spread over his face. "So let me get this straight. You found Mysterio in an alley, he handed you the dragon and then the cape attacked and killed him."

I swung one leg over the opposite knee. "Sounds about right. Oh, and I tried to save him. I didn't want him to die. I never want anyone to die. Dying is not good."

He stared at me blankly.

I sat on my hands to keep from twisting my fingers together. "I talk when I get nervous."

"Do you have something to be nervous about?"

I shook my head. "No. Nothing to be nervous about. Not really. No. Maybe it's because you're so tall and I'm just average."

"But we're sitting."

I nodded. "I know. It doesn't make any sense, I realize. It just is."

"Is there anything else you ladies would like to add to your statements?"

I shook my head of hair, letting some of the strands fall on my face. "Nope. Nothing."

Betty nodded. "Same here. I've told you coppers everything you need to know."

Garrick's lips tipped into an amused smile. He rose and gestured toward the door. "Thank you, ladies. We'll be in contact if there's more we need help with."

Betty huffed all the way outside. "Coppers always getting into my business and things. All of them. Every one."

"I think you're exaggerating." I glanced at my watch and realized I was supposed to have had dinner with Axel. I palmed my forehead and exhaled in defeat. "Oh no. Axel doesn't know we were at the police station. He'll think I stood him up."

"Where's your phone?" Betty said.

I grimaced. "It must be at the house. We dashed out, remember?"

Betty handed the cage to me. "Here. You're younger and stronger than me."

"Thanks," I mumbled. I stared at the peaceful face of the sleeping dragon. He was so cute. You would never think he could scorch your skin black.

We reached the house a few minutes later. I snatched my phone from my purse.

"It rang while you were gone," Amelia said.

A knot of butterflies whipped up a storm in my gut. "Great."

I went upstairs to my room, where I set the dragon on the floor. I glanced at my phone and saw that I'd missed one phone call from Axel. I immediately dialed his number but got his voicemail.

I sank onto the bed. "Awesome. I was going to have a real date with this guy—not walking around a festival and not on a covert dinner mission, but an actual date where there's no drama, but I blew it."

Mattie jumped from the window seat. "It'll be okay, sugar. Promise."

I rubbed behind her ears as I let the night's events sink into my muscles. "Can you think of anything my mom would've wanted to tell me? Something secret and private? Something she couldn't say to anyone else?"

Mattie yawned and stretched her legs. "Naw, there's nothin' I can think of that your momma wouldn't have said aloud to someone."

"Hmm."

"You don't believe me."

I shook my head from side to side. "It's not that I don't believe you. It's more that Mysterio said she'd given him a message and he'd written it down."

The cat blinked. "Well, where is it?"

"That's what I don't know. The police have his van, so it's not like I can search it. Unless…"

Mattie poked me in the leg. "Unless what?"

I sat up. "Unless Mysterio accidentally left something at the inn."

I shot off the bed and padded to Cordelia's room. I knocked softly. "Come in."

She thumbed off her phone when I entered. A huge grin had spread across her face, and she was practically glowing.

I leaned against the doorjamb. "Your new boyfriend?"

Cordelia rolled her eyes. "I'm not saying anything that might incriminate me."

I chuckled. "Probably a good thing since you live under Betty's roof. All you've got to do is *think* the wrong thing and you're guilty of something."

Cordelia winked. "Sounds about right."

Several days ago my cousin had been dressed up for what looked like a date. She vehemently refused to admit that's what she was doing, and though I suspected, I still had no idea who she'd gone out with. Cordelia wasn't talking and I wasn't about to push her on the subject because basically, it wasn't my business.

"I need a favor," I said.

She tossed her phone on the comforter and stretched out her legs. "What favor would that be?"

I eased forward and shut the door softly behind me. "Do you think anyone's cleaned Mysterio's room yet?"

Cordelia inspected a strand of her hair before tucking it behind one ear. "Doubt it. That won't be done until the morning. Why?"

"Because I need to get in there."

Our gazes locked. "Um. *Why?*"

I cracked the knuckles on my right hand nervously. I'd never asked my cousin for a favor like this. I didn't want to get her into trouble and I also didn't want to put any kind of strain on our relationship, but I had to.

"Because I think he might've left behind my mother's message. When I asked him about it earlier, you know before he died, he started to say he'd written it down." I crossed my fingers. "I'm hoping he left a notebook or a pad or something in that room."

Cordelia nibbled her bottom lip.

I threaded my fingers together as if in prayer. "Please. I have to know what she wanted to tell me. I know y'all think he was a charlatan, and he might've been. But that image of my mother—" I shook my head and swallowed the tears threatening to stream from my eyes, "—that figure of her looked real. And if she had something she needed to tell me? I have to know what that is. I just have to."

A wall of pressure built up in my chest. I felt like I was going to burst—like a geyser of pain-laden tears would gush from me.

Cordelia rose and wrapped me in her arms. "It's okay. I can get you into his room."

Hope blossomed in my chest. "You can?"

She smiled warmly. "I can. Just don't cry on me."

I laughed. "I'll do my best."

Cordelia slung her purse over one shoulder and said, "Grab your stuff. There won't be much staff at the inn right now. Let's go see if Mysterio left anything behind."

WE RODE our skillets to the inn and left them at what could be considered a bike rack, except it was for cast iron riding skillets.

I leaned mine on its pan end and tied it to the steel frame. "That's nifty."

Cordelia tugged a rope around the handle of hers. "Comes in handy."

I followed her inside. Behind the desk was a sour-looking, twenty-something young woman. The sides of her head were shaved and she'd styled her thick red hair into what looked like a tidal wave that appeared to be about to crash over the left side of her head. I stared at her hair, wondering what sort of product she'd used to get it to shape that way.

"If you take a picture it'll last longer," she snapped.

I grimaced, embarrassed that I'd been caught. "Sorry. But your hair is so cool. I was trying to figure out how you'd done that."

She gave me a hard look and said, "Magic," as if I was too stupid to live.

I cleared my throat and stared at the floor. "Sure. I should've known." Well, it looked like I was properly chastened for being an idiot.

Cordelia stepped behind the counter. "Bree, this is my cousin Pepper."

Bree snorted. "Oh right. The newbie witch. I should've known."

Cordelia reached across Bree. "Isn't there a new sheet we're supposed to follow for ordering supplies?"

Bree thumbed toward a closet. "I put it in back."

"Can you grab it for me? I need to put something down."

Bree rolled her eyes, but she opened the door and proceeded to grab what Cordelia asked. I watched as Cordelia snatched a room key from the wall and tucked it into her pants. Bree returned and Cordelia gave her a big smile.

"Thanks so much," she said, scribbling something on the paper. "Pepper, I'll show you around the place before we leave."

I followed Cordelia around the corner. She took a side staircase up one floor to a hall with several doors. She pushed the key into a lock and winced as the hinges creaked.

"Bree has great hearing," she whispered. We entered and Cordelia quietly closed the door behind us. "One time she actually heard an employee stealing bath supplies from the closet. Heard the woman tucking them into her purse and then confronted her when the cleaning lady was in the parking lot. Bree got her fired."

"She was stealing," I said.

"The woman was in her seventies and on a fixed income," Cordelia said. "Maybe she needed some extra soap."

"Maybe she was selling it on the black market."

Cordelia smirked. "Not likely." She fisted her hands to her hips. "So this was Mysterio's room."

My gaze swept over the floral print chair tucked into one corner, the desk nestled beside a small window and the bed with a simple floral quilt thrown atop.

"Not a lot here," I said, already disappointed.

Cordelia opened the dresser drawers. "I was afraid of that, but you never know."

I moved to the desk. Sitting on the shiny surface sat an ashtray with a snubbed out cigar inside.

"Did Mysterio smoke?"

Cordelia didn't look up. "No clue. But this is a non-smoking room."

The desk drawers slid open with ease. Except for one Bible, they were all empty. I crossed to the chair, but there was nothing in the seat and nothing on the floor. I moved to the bathroom, but other than a mound of wet towels, I didn't see anything there, either.

"What's this?" Cordelia said.

I found her standing over the bed with one of the inn's notepads in her hand. "You found something?"

She turned around. "Look at it."

My cousin displayed a pad with the inn's letterhead. It had been ripped at the bottom, but a few words remained at the top.

Tell her that though we are separated—

The rest had been cut off. My hopes faded until I realized that the bottom of the next page had writing indentions on it. The words had been pressed in as if Mysterio were angry when he wrote. I ran my fingers over the impression.

I flipped up the page. The words at the top of the page didn't press into the next one, but the words at the bottom were dented.

Meaning, the top message hadn't been written hard enough for me to figure out what it was by looking at the page underneath it.

I didn't know if the words at the bottom were connected to those at the top—the ones that appeared to be written about me, but since the page had been ripped off, it made me think that whatever had been written was incredibly important.

Maybe worth killing for.

Was I jumping to conclusions?

Possibly. But sometimes jumping to conclusions kept you alive, or so I liked to think.

"What do you think?" Cordelia said.

"It looks like Mysterio wrote a message below that was important.

Think we can do a rubbing or some magic and figure out what it says?"

She licked her lips. "Yeah. But let's get to the house. If I'm discovered in this room, I'll be fired."

I crinkled my nose. "Why?"

Cordelia snapped off a light. "Because unless we need to be in a room, we're not supposed to be. Plus, this guy was murdered and the police haven't checked in here yet. That alone could get me fired. Come on."

I tucked the notepad into my purse and headed for the door. I reached out to grab the knob and watched as it turned from the other side.

The door creaked open as my heart thundered in my chest.

Crap.

Looked like Cordelia and I were dead meat.

SEVEN

The door opened. I shrank like a school kid about to be sent to the principal's office.

"What are y'all doing here?"

The husky voice took me by surprise, but when I looked into Axel's ocean blue eyes, I was relieved. "Thank God," I said. "I thought we were in trouble."

He shifted his weight. "The police are about to be here, so you might be in trouble if you don't scat."

I flashed him a huge grin. "Thanks."

Cordelia slinked past me. "I need to return this key."

"I didn't hear that," Axel said.

"Then you didn't see this either," she said as she locked the door.

"Sure didn't."

Cordelia touched my arm. "See you at the house."

"Okay."

She walked off. I pulled my hair over one shoulder and twisted it. "I'm sorry about our dinner date. See, I came to talk to Mysterio, but he was murdered by his own cape."

"I heard already. I tried calling you."

My gaze dropped to the floor. "I tried calling you back. I figured you found somebody else to take out."

He chuckled. The corners of his eyes crinkled. "Not a chance. Come on. Let's get off this floor before the police arrive."

"I'm surprised they hadn't checked his room already."

Axel raked his fingers through his hair. "I think they've been busy with other things."

I frowned. "What other things?"

He smirked. "Police stuff."

"Very cryptic."

"I'm a cryptic kind of guy...You hungry?"

I thought about it for a moment. "Yeah. I could use some food."

"I know a great little place not far from here."

I grabbed my skillet and we strolled downtown toward what looked like a hot dog stand with picnic tables sprinkled around it.

We found an empty table under a magnolia tree. The humid night air was thick with the sounds of frogs croaking and crickets chirping. What appeared to be a glowing moth flitted around my head. I brushed the insect away.

"Darlin' if you don't want me taking your order, you can go eat somewhere else."

I blinked. "What was that?"

Axel motioned toward the moth. "That's Pixie, the pixie. She's the waitress and owner of the pop-up food stand."

"Whoa. What?"

Axel chuckled. "They come by every once in a while. Serve the best barbecue pulled pork sandwiches around. Trust me on this."

Pixie flitted to me. "I'm so sorry," I said. "I had no idea that you were a pixie. And alive. And breathing. And flying. Sorry. I talk a lot when I get nervous."

Pixie fluttered up beside us. "Don't apologize. I'll be taking your order, is all. What'll it be?"

I dipped my head toward Axel. "Order for me. Whatever you want. I'll eat it up."

Axel's grin spread wide. He drummed his fingers on the table and said, "We'll have two sandwiches with baked beans, corn fritters and blackberry cobbler for dessert."

My eyes widened. "Wow. That sounds awesome."

"It is," Pixie said, buzzing around us. "It'll be coming right up."

The pixie left and I sank my head onto the table. "I'm so embarrassed. This whole magical being thing is taking some getting used to."

He squeezed my arm. A jolt of heat snaked up my flesh. "You'll get used to it. It'll take some time." Our gazes locked. My stomach coiled from nerves. "So what were you looking for in Mysterio's room?"

I shot him a coy smile. "Who says I was looking for anything?"

"I do."

"Right. Okay. I didn't have a chance to tell you, but last night Mysterio brought forth an image of my mother."

Axel's eyes narrowed. "She was one of the figures who appeared?"

I braided my hair over one shoulder. "Yeah. But that's not all. He also told me that she had a message for me. But it was private, one he could only tell me later."

"Where? In his hotel room?"

"I take it from your tone you think he was full of crap."

Axel's shoulders sank. "You said yourself the guy was with a different woman every five minutes."

"I don't think I said that exactly."

"Close enough. To answer your question—yes, I think Mysterio wanted to get you alone."

I propped my elbows on the table and sank my chin onto one palm. "So what about the image of my mother? How do you explain that?"

Axel took my free hand in his. He turned it over as if learning the lines and creases. "I don't. I can't explain how Mysterio performs his show. Does he use some sort of magical projector with images already pre-recorded? He *does* perform in small towns. The populations of which are well known to anyone in city hall, for instance. He could have a contact and they could tell him about the residents, give him what information he needs. Then all Mysterio has to do is some research, figure out who his target's deceased loved ones are, and make some magic happen."

I quirked a brow. "Have you done this before? You seem knowledgeable."

He chuckled. "No, but scam artists are scam artists. Some do meticulous research on their marks."

"You're saying Mysterio picked me for some reason and then created the image and the story that my mother had more to tell me?"

Axel's finger lit a trail of fire down my arm. "I'm saying it's one possibility."

A tray of food arrived with Pixie the pixie holding it up with her hands. She looked like a tiny superhero carrying the world on her shoulders.

"Let me help you with that," Axel said. He took the tray and dished out our food.

The smoky scent of hickory wafted up from the sandwiches. "That smells like heaven," I said.

"It is," she said. "Heaven between a bun and in a cobbler. Y'all enjoy. Holler if you need anything."

We dug into our sandwiches. Sweet juicy barbecue sauce left a wonderful vinegar tang on my tongue. I chewed and swallowed, stopping myself from gorging on the meal.

"Oh wait," I said. I dropped the sandwich, cleaned my fingers and pulled the notepad from my purse. "We found this in Mysterio's room."

Axel closed his eyes. "A room the police haven't gone through yet."

"You snooze. You lose." I sniffed it. "And boy, does it smell like cigar smoke."

A crease formed between Axel's brows. "Cigar?"

"Yep." I slid it over to him. "Look at that."

"It appears to be a message."

I jammed my finger on top. "To me. That message is to me."

"And you know this how?"

I lifted my nose and said, "I feel it in my bones."

"You're too young to have arthritis."

43

"That's not true. Some people get arthritis when they're young."

Axel shot me a dark look. "I know you don't have it. So you're too young."

"Stop making fun of me. Seriously. This note is about whatever my mother wanted me to know and it's been ripped off. Why?"

Axel sighed. He took the paper and studied it. "There are impressions on the bottom half."

I was so excited I nearly bit my lip to bleeding. "Yes. I know. That's the clue we need."

"The clue to what?"

I scooped baked beans into my mouth and chewed for a moment. Wonderful brown sugar and bacon hit my tongue. Wow. Seriously. I could eat this food every day of the week. "That's the clue we need to figure out the original message."

His lips curved into a sly smile. "And just what exactly are you thinking?"

I cleared my throat. "I don't know. Either Mysterio wrote something super important on the bottom half and ripped it off. Or..."

"Yes, Detective Dunn? Don't leave me in suspense," he said.

I scowled. The delicious smile on his lips made my hormones sing. "Or Mysterio wrote something important and someone stole it, taking my half of the message with it. We uncover what the message is and maybe I can find out what it was my mother wanted me to know."

"So that's what this is all about?"

I swallowed an emotional knot in my throat. "Yes. She wanted to tell me something. I can't let this opportunity pass me by, Axel. I have to know." My gaze drifted to the table. "I never met her. For once in my life—living here in Magnolia Cove, I have the chance to learn things about her, things my father never shared with me before he passed. I want as much information as I can get."

Axel studied me. He squinted as if trying to decipher if I was telling the truth. His lips formed a thin line and he slowly nodded. "What would you like to do?"

I licked my lips. "Can you do a rubbing or some magic to figure out what was on the sheet? Is that possible?"

Axel dragged his gaze to the pad. He ran his thumb over the indentions and said, "I'm pretty sure we can." He glanced at the table of food between us. "In fact, we've got the right ingredients."

My gaze swept over the sandwiches, baked beans, cobbler and sweet teas. Nothing on the table made me think about magic or what we could use.

I cocked a brow. "And what exactly is going to help us with this?"

Axel smiled wide. "Why, the blackberries, of course."

I nearly facepalmed my forehead. "Of course. The blackberries. Makes perfect sense. Why didn't I think of that?"

He winked at me mischievously. "You just haven't been around magic as long as I have. That's all. Don't worry. I'll save some of my cobbler and when we leave here, we'll see what we can find out."

It took everything I had not to shovel the rest of my food in my mouth. Actually, I probably did heave it in there because the food was so darned delicious.

Axel paid and we slipped into the Mustang.

"So where are we off to?" I said.

"The Potion Pools are a great spot for this type of work. Come on. We'll see what we can conjure up there."

I felt my lips curl. I'd witnessed Axel do a smattering of magic, but that was all. I'd never watched him perform what I could only describe as a full on spell, or even magic that consisted of actually seeing his power. My stomach quivered in anticipation.

We wound around and down into a small valley nestled at the base below downtown. A copse of magnolia trees surrounded a sparkling pond. Moonlight glinted off the surface, making the water shine like diamonds.

A creek trickled into the pool and at the center, the water babbled as if a small fountain lived at the base.

I slid from the seat. A cool breeze pricked my skin and lifted the hair from my nape. I inhaled the sweet scent of magnolia blossoms. I heard a snap and glanced to see Axel extending a bloom for me.

"Sweet for a sweet," he said.

"Thank you."

Our gazes locked and heat dotted my cheeks. I bit my lip and glanced away. My skin tingled and sang, but I needed to focus on business. Not on how hot Axel looked and how I wanted to lose myself in his beautiful blue eyes.

"Is it too much? The flower? I can take it back."

My eyes widened. "No. Why would you say that?"

His gaze darted across the landscape. "Only because you look like you're about to be sick."

I tipped a shoulder into a half-shrug. "It's nothing. Just, you know, feelings and stuff."

"Feelings? You have those?"

I elbowed his ribs. "Only a few."

He led me to a bench beside the pool and opened the to-go container with the cobbler. "There's a spell that uses fruit to reveal missing words on a page."

I leaned back on my palms. "I don't know what kind of wizard you are. I'm a head witch, Betty's a kitchen witch—what are you?"

Axel rubbed a thumb over his brow. "I'm a jack-of-all-trades wizard. I can do a little of everything."

I tipped my head toward him. "And by a little bit of everything you mean?"

He coughed into his fist. "I mean I can use earth energy, I can summon creatures if need be. I can suck a person's power if I have to. I can even use another witch's magic against them."

My throat dried. "Holy heck. And y'all said being a head witch is the most powerful kind of witch there is. I don't have anything compared to that."

Axel chuckled. "You can do more because the only thing that limits you is your mind. I'm limited by ingredients, situations, whatever's in front of me. You're not limited by anything and until you learn to accept that, you'll be limiting yourself."

I shifted. "Is that true?"

"Would I lie to you?"

"You didn't tell me you were a werewolf."

Axel scowled. "For your protection. There will always be things I do for your protection. Things you may not understand, but are necessary."

"Cryptic yet again." I flicked a strand of hair over my shoulder. "I like living dangerously."

He leaned so close our lips were almost touching. "Are you trying to seduce me?"

I blinked and backed away. "No. No. Not seducing. Sorry. I wasn't trying to seem like that. I don't know. I think it's this magnolia blossom. The scent's so sweet. It's wonderful. Puts me in a romantic mood."

Axel's lips coiled. "Happens to lots of folks at the pools...Do you remember why you're here?"

I cleared my throat and straightened my spine. "For my mother."

"Right. Let's see what we can see."

Axel twirled a finger. The glob of blackberries wiggled out from under the shell of cobbler and lifted into the night air. They twirled and gyrated, coiling into a tight cylinder. The syrupy concoction broke apart into seeds and black fruit.

My jaw fell as Axel continued motioning with his hand effortlessly and the fruit continued to bend to his power.

"The notepad?"

I fished it from my purse and placed it in his open palm. The blackberries, in their tight coil, ascended into the air. With a twitch of his fingers, the fruit dove onto the pad, splashing as if they were dunking below the surface of a pool.

Axel twirled his finger again and a line of water sprang up from the pool, descending onto the page with a flourish.

I inhaled a shot of air, only then realizing that I'd been holding my breath. "What does it show?"

Axel stared at the sheet for a long moment before turning it toward me. I frowned. The fruit had spilled perfectly into the nooks and crevices of the impressions, but what they revealed took a moment to register.

"It's an address," I said. "Three hundred Fairy Lane. Is that what it looks like to you?"

Axel agreed. He tugged his phone from his pocket and thumbed it to life. "It's a shop address. Fairy Lane is here, in Magnolia Cove."

"What store does it belong to?"

He frowned at the map. "Spellin' Skillet."

I gnawed the inside of my mouth. That wasn't right. Something about that address didn't ring true. Then it hit me.

"It's not an address for Spellin' Skillet. It's for Witch's Wardrobe, the store next to it."

Axel's brows pinched together. "What makes you say that?"

I cracked the knuckles on my right hand. "For several reasons—the first is that Gretchen Gargoyle left with Mysterio the night of his performance. She interrupted my meeting with him—you know, the one where I was supposed to find out the secret my mother wanted me to know."

"And the second?"

"The second is the most suspect," I said. "It's the fact that Mysterio died at the hands of his cape and if there's one witch in town with power over fabric, it's Gretchen Gargoyle. Which means—"

"—Miss Gargoyle may have killed Mysterio."

I nodded. "And more important, she might've stolen this note. So if she also holds the rest of the paper, she knows the message my mother wanted me to know." I narrowed my gaze. "That's one secret I intend to find out."

EIGHT

*a*s much as I wanted to track Gretchen Gargoyle down that very night and pester the heck out of her about that note, Axel didn't let me.

He curbed the car in front of Betty's house. "We'll talk to her tomorrow."

"Are you sure? I think maybe Gretchen wouldn't mind letting us in for coffee while I raked her over the coals about the note she clearly stole."

Axel chuckled. "Quite the imagination you've got on you."

"I thought you were going to say mouth."

His gaze slid to mine, spearing my heart to my spine. I sucked air as Axel's lips ticked up. "You've certainly got one of those on you as well."

"In a good way?"

He leaned over and gently grazed his mouth across mine. A light moan escaped me. When we parted he said, "Yes. In a good way."

I smiled and Axel escorted me to the door. I kissed his cheek and told him not to bother coming in. He promised to call the next day, before we planned on talking to Gretchen.

I'm pretty sure he realized that if he spoke to her without me, I'd be pretty p-o'd at him.

I patted Jennie the guard-vine before entering a quiet house. For once, Betty wasn't waiting up for me with a shotgun strapped across her knees. Perhaps I'd proven myself worthy of not needing a grandmother for a babysitter.

Or maybe Betty was simply too tired to stay up.

It was probably that one.

I climbed the stairs to my room. I found Mattie curled on my comforter. I changed and slipped underneath the bedding. A whimper had me glancing around the room. In the corner lay the dragon in his cage.

"Oh, little guy. I forgot all about you."

The dragon thumped his tail.

"Betty cleaned his cage."

I looked over to see Mattie staring at me with one green eye open.

"That was nice of her."

"Sure was," Mattie said, "because it sure did stink. You gotta potty train that dragon."

I scoffed. "As if."

Mattie closed her eyes and snuggled into a tight ball. "I'm sure it can be done."

"Good night, y'all," I said.

And with that, I fell into a dreamless sleep.

The next morning, Betty left breakfast for the three of us.

"Wow," I said, clapping my hands together. "Chocolate gravy, biscuits and eggs. This is awesome."

Cordelia licked a finger she'd dredged in the sauce. "Nothing better than chocolate for breakfast."

"You got that right," Amelia said.

I poured a big dollop of gravy over my biscuits. Now, it might be called chocolate gravy, which sounds disgusting, but it's actually a chocolate sauce concocted from cocoa powder, sugar, flour, milk and butter. It's freaking amazing. Nothing like it on earth.

I moaned as the chocolate and biscuit hit my tongue. I opened my

eyes and saw my cousins laughing at me. Deciding not to acknowl-
edge their amusement, I said, "Did you have any trouble returning
the key?"

Cordelia shook her head. "Not at all."

"What key?" Amelia said.

Cordelia poked at her food. "I let Pepper into Mysterio's room
ahead of the police."

"You did? Wow, that's so un-straight and narrow. Completely
unlike you."

Cordelia flashed Amelia a tight smile. "I can let my hair down now
and then."

Amelia sipped her coffee. "I'd love to see it."

"What is this, a challenge—like truth or dare?"

Amelia glowed with interest. "Sure. Truth or Dare. Want to play?"

"No."

"Party pooper."

"Girls, let's be nice. Remember we love each other," I said.

Amelia laughed. "One day. One day we'll get Cordelia not to be so
serious."

I quirked a brow. I had a feeling my cousin Cordelia was a lot less
serious than any of us thought. The fact that she had a secret love
interest proved the fact to me.

"So how's Zach?" I said.

Cordelia choked on her biscuit. "Good. He's good. Still studying
that ancient culture."

"When do you expect him home?" I said.

Amelia poured creamer into a fresh cup of coffee. "Oh, Zach's
never coming home. In the three years that he and Cordelia have been
dating, he's only ever come to Magnolia Cove once."

Cordelia bristled. "He's busy."

Amelia stirred the cup. "He is very busy. So busy I've forgotten
what he looks like."

Cordelia shrugged. "I haven't."

I wiped the corner of my mouth and dropped the napkin on the
table. "Do y'all need help cleaning up?"

Cordelia snapped her fingers. "We're sweet tea witches, Pepper. I'll have this mess cleaned up in a snap. Don't worry about it."

I thanked her and gathered my purse and dragon to take to work. I draped the cage as I didn't want a thousand people asking questions about the creature—either on my way to work or when I got there. I figured the fewer people who knew about him, the better.

'Course, I still had to figure out what the heck I was going to do with the creature.

I arrived at Familiar Place and tidied up before it was doors-open time. I had just brushed a bit of dirt from my hands when the door swung wide.

My jaw fell.

Standing in the frame stood a man wearing lederhosen, except minus the white shirt—and it appeared the lederhosen were made from leather.

Okay.

My brain hiccupped. I blinked, making sure my eyes weren't deceiving me.

Yes, in the doorway of my shop stood a grown man built like Hercules wearing leather lederhosen—basically shorts with suspenders and a bar strapped over the chest.

"Hello?" I said, totally confused.

"I am Barry," the man said, striding in. His stone-like thighs were so large he walked like a pro-wrestler; legs splayed wide, his feet landing about two people apart.

I cocked my head so far my neck popped. Oh yes, that felt good. "Barry?"

A short figure busted in around him. "Barry the Dragon Tamer."

Betty Craple fisted her hands to her hips and nodded proudly. "He came all the way from Las Vegas, where he has a show on the Magic Strip."

"The Magic Strip?"

Betty pulled a pipe from her pocket and packed a wad of tobacco in it. "That's where all the witches go for the magical shows. You can't expect Barry to perform with dragons where any Joe Schmoe could see, do you?"

She had me there. "I guess not."

Barry strode in and fisted his hands to his hips. "I hear there is a dragon in this righteous town of Magnolia Cove."

"Um. Yeah. I've got one."

Barry leaned back as if faking surprise. "Allow me to see the creature. Peer into its eyes of death."

I shot Betty an are-you-serious look as I crossed to the cage. I unfurled the covering.

"Behold, I witness the fire-breather," Barry said.

Unable to stand it any longer, I waved toward Betty. "Does he always talk like this?"

"Barry, you can knock off the act. She's not buying it."

Barry knelt to eye level with the dragon. The beast thumped its tail. "Well lookie here," Barry said. "What you've got in that there cage has got to be one of the beautiest looking dragons I ever did see."

Beautiest?

I yawned. "Never mind. I prefer if he talks the other way."

Barry laughed. "It's all an act. I like to be funny. Liven things up. A little majesty in my speech never hurt anybody, and it sure didn't hurt me. But let me take a look at this creature."

Barry slicked a hand over his short, sleek dark hair. "You know there are only one hundred known dragons in all the world."

"That would make him one hundred and one," Betty said proudly.

"It's not like it's your great-grandchild or anything," I said.

She sniffed. "I'm still proud."

Barry glanced over his shoulder at me. "I have five myself. Dragons don't often live long in captivity, so whoever bought this one probably had to prove that the dragon would be well cared for."

"My deceased great-uncle," I said.

Barry rose. "He's young, and this pup needs help if you're to mold him, shape him into the king dragon he should be. I can see it now." He raised a hand and traced some imaginary voyage with his gaze. "This young beast becomes the mightiest of all dragons, slaying anyone or anything with intentions to attack you. You can fly on its back, sailing the skies and the world. You, Pepper Dunn, will be a princess among dragons."

"Um. Okay," I said, slowly backing away. "But for now, can we just make sure it's potty trained and maybe teach it not to shoot fire at people?"

A smile flared on Barry's face. "We can do that and so much more."

Interest sparked in my core. "Oh? Like what else?"

Barry grinned. "First things first. Grab some mice. You've got to learn to feed it."

AGAINST MY BETTER DESIRES, though definitely not judgments, I boxed up a couple of mice. Barry grabbed the cage while Betty greeted customers and promised to watch the shop while I was gone.

"Can't we do this tomorrow? When the store's closed?"

Barry *tsked*. "Time is of the essence. You must bond with the dragon, and the dragon to you. It's important for all other aspects of your relationship. The creature's feeding is prime time to build this bond."

Great. "Do I have to watch?"

"Yes."

Double great.

I followed Barry down Bubbling Cauldron and past the Potion Pools, where Axel and I had been just the previous night. Behind the copse of magnolias was a large field. There were some kids playing ball and witches practicing spells. Orbs of magic floated around along with common objects like balls and pens.

"We may need something a bit more private for this," Barry said.

He clapped his hands. Green walls shot up around us. They grew tall and fast, rumbling from the earth. It was like we were enclosed in a giant maze.

I stumbled. "What's going on?"

Barry watched until the walls stopped. "This is what I call privacy.

You need it when training dragons. They can become distracted easily. Hunt the wrong prey, that sort of thing."

"And here I was worried the dragon would charge after one of those kids."

Barry pouched out his bottom lip. "Not a concern at this moment. If the dragon was a bit older and untrained, maybe. But right now you're safe."

I scoffed. "Good to know."

Barry stalked around our magical fortress. "Before we begin, there are certain things you need to know about the creature that will now be with you."

I gulped. "Like what?"

"Dragons bond for life, for one. So once the bond is formed, it will seal the two of you. It will be a familiar and witch relationship."

I crossed my arms. "What if we don't bond?"

Barry grazed his fingers over the cage. "Then you have a mistress/beast relationship; it just isn't at the same level."

"Will the dragon try to fricassee me?"

Barry laughed. "Probably not."

"Probably? You're not making me feel confident, here."

"I can't lie and say otherwise."

"What else?" I grumbled, not feeling particularly confident in how this dragon was going to fit into the rest of my life.

"Dragons are as loyal as dogs. You'll find this creature to be one of the best out there. They can be a little wild, but they love to serve. Now, let's open up the cage and get you two bonding."

Barry clicked the lock. The door swung wide and the dragon stretched. It batted its eyes at me, yawned and said, "Mama."

Barry reached inside and pulled the creature out. He hoisted it onto his shoulder, where the dragon curled around his neck.

"This is a pose they love when they're young. I encourage you to let your dragon sit like this whenever you have free time."

I snickered. "You mean like when I'm watching TV?"

Barry's eyes brightened. "Exactly."

Yeah. That's not going to happen.

Barry scratched under its chin. "What's this little guy's name?"

"Uh, I don't know. Dragon?"

Barry laughed. It was high pitched and the complete opposite of his macho man exterior. "That's not an original name."

I cracked my knuckles. "To be honest, I didn't want him until my grandmother told me about the whole protecting thing. I don't know what his name is—Fire Breather? Sally? I have no clue what to name him."

Barry's eyes sparkled with delight. "He will tell you his name."

"In that case, his name must be 'Mama' because that's what he says whenever he sees me."

"Ah, so the connection has started. The two of you are linked. Wonderful. Now, let us start the real training. Take one of the mice from the box and hold it by the tail."

I grimaced, but I did as he asked, taking one of the mice. "I don't like cruelty to any animals."

Barry stroked the dragon. "You're thinking of this the entirely wrong way. This is the life cycle. That little mouse isn't dying in vain. It's feeding this dragon that will protect and help you. You must think big picture. Not be so small in your mind."

"Okay, I won't be so small in mind," I said sarcastically, tossing a strand of hair over my shoulder.

Barry clapped and a leather glove similar to one a falconer would wear appeared over my outstretched hand. I still dangled the mouse, but now I had the glove over it.

"Call the dragon," he said.

"Come here, boy. Get some food."

The dragon opened one eye and stared at me. Then it closed its eye and sighed, snuggling against Barry.

"You must command the creature," Barry said. "Command him. Tell him to come."

Feeling like a great fool, I said, "Come!"

The dragon blinked both eyes open this time, but sank back to his nap.

A bit perturbed and feeling embarrassed that I wasn't bossy and commanding the way I wanted to be, I reached into the very pit of my belly, opened my mouth and said in the most pointed way ever, "Get your rear end off him and get over here and eat this mouse. If you don't, I will never feed you again."

The dragon's eyes snapped open. In one, two, three seconds, he uncoiled from Barry and flew straight toward me.

I closed my eyes and cringed as the creature swooped. I felt a tug as it took the mouse. Wings beat hard, fluttering my hair. I opened my eyes.

The baby dragon hovered before me. It was completely outstretched, the scales on its belly flaunting gorgeous jewel tones of purple and green. It flapped its wings and stretched its neck toward the sky.

The dragon howled. A stream of fire shot from its mouth before petering out.

The creature looked directly at me and said, "Mama."

A smile tugged at the corners of my lips. "Mama," I agreed.

"You must name him now," Barry said. "That will help the bond you're creating."

As the dragon stared at me, I sensed him reaching out with his mind, felt him magically touch my power and noticed a flare in my core. My power stirred. For a moment, I felt complete control. It was like the pairing of this dragon to me would help me harness and control the magic. For the first time since learning of my power, I had the feeling I was in control of my magic, instead of it being the other way around.

I reached for the creature. My fingers glowed. The dragon sank toward my hand and I touched its head. A halo of power swept along my arms and up my throat, blanketing me in a warm cocoon of magic.

The name came to me as if the dragon had fed it into my mind. "Hugo?"

The dragon shot back and away, sailing up before plummeting to perch on my shoulder like a parrot on a pirate.

I wobbled, balancing under the added weight.

Barry laughed. "I think he likes the name."

As if to agree with his point, the dragon opened its mouth and shot a line of fire into the air.

"Ah yes," Barry said. "That is the name."

I nibbled my bottom lip. "I sure hope so, because I certainly don't want to end up burned toast."

Barry crossed to me and pulled the glove from my hand. "Oh, they don't generally shoot fire in their sleep."

I wiped my hand over my forehead in relief. "That's good to know."

Barry stopped. "I said, generally. It could happen."

Great. Just one more thing to worry about.

NINE

"So why are you walking around with a dragon on your neck?"

It was late afternoon. Axel had picked me up on his way to Witch's Wardrobe.

I sighed. "We're supposed to be bonding."

Mischief danced in his blue eyes. "I don't think you're going to fit into the truck that way."

He'd left the Mustang at home for the day and was patiently waiting for me to slip inside the single cab pickup.

"I could ride my skillet over."

Axel raked his knuckles over his jaw. "I don't have mine anymore."

I squinted at him. "You got something against skillets?"

"They're more for the ladies than for me."

I laughed. "Not manly enough for you, huh? Would you like a dragon around your neck?"

"I'd take that over a flying skillet."

I pulled Hugo from my shoulders. "He can sit in my lap."

The dragon did. Rode just like a doggie in mommy's lap all the way to Witch's Wardrobe.

As the store came into view, I gnawed the inside of my lip before spitting it out. "Gretchen was pretty ticked at me last time I was here. Said she'd kick me out if I ever came in again."

Axel slid into a spot and killed the engine. "You're with me. She won't be kicking anyone out of her store."

I placed a hand over my heart. "Great, 'cause I was so worried."

"No, you weren't. You were joking."

I smiled widely. "Maybe."

We strolled inside and found Gretchen sorting an assortment of Flutter Dresses. A Flutter Dress, as I found out not long ago, is supposed to help a person be better at a specific task—like dancing. Of course, nothing works out easy for me. I got stuck inside a dress and couldn't break free. I do blame my aunts—mischief witches extraordinaire. They were currently lying low since last week's fiasco with the festival. But I knew they'd return.

Anyway, in my attempt to rid myself of the dress, I nearly destroyed Gretchen's store. So she kinda dislikes me.

I don't suppose I blame her.

Gretchen smiled when her gaze settled on Axel. She frowned when she saw me, though her eyes flared at the sight of Hugo wrapped around my neck.

"Is that a dragon?" she said, her hands flailing in total fan girl mode.

I clicked my tongue. "It sure is. Would you like to pet him?"

She wiggled her fingers. "Yes. I would love to pet him. What's his name?"

"Um. Hugo."

Hugo's gaze flickered to me as if to ask if I needed something.

"He's beautiful," she said.

"Thank you."

Gretchen's brows pinched together and her lips pursed, making me think she hadn't exactly forgiven me for nearly wrecking her shop.

While she stroked the dragon, Axel started the questioning. "It's terrible about Mysterio, isn't it?"

Gretchen sucked her lower lip. "I would say that it is."

I pressed Hugo into her arms and decided to play stupid. "It's horrible, really. I don't know if you attended the show but my mother's spirit appeared and Mysterio said she had a message for me. I went to his dressing room to get it, but he ended up leaving for dinner." I smacked my palm to my forehead. "Oh my gosh, that's right! You came in and picked him up." I grabbed her arm as if we were best friends. "Are you okay? You must've been so close to him. Oh, I'm so sorry."

Gretchen sniffled and hugged Hugo to her. A bit brave, if you ask me. If I'd just met a dragon, I sure as heck wouldn't be embracing him as if he were a toy poodle.

"It's okay, really. I'm thankful I met Mysterio and had the chance to spend the time with him that I did. It wasn't a lifetime, but it was worth it."

I shot Axel a look. So had they been lovers?

"He must've been a great boyfriend," I said. "He seemed like it, and you don't appear to be the jealous type at all."

Gretchen's mouth ticked up. "Mysterio had a lot of love to dish out. So much love can't be contained for just one person."

"So you let him sleep around," Axel said.

My eyes widened. "Why not just cut to the chase?"

"What's the point?" He glanced at Gretchen. "We're trying to track down what exactly Pepper's mother wanted her to know. We found a notepad of Mysterio's with this address on it along with a partial note from Pepper's mom, or so it appears."

Gretchen handed Hugo to me. "Why wouldn't he have had this address? We saw each other every time he came into town."

Axel traced a thumb across his lower lip. "But why would he *need* it? Wouldn't he have known it by heart? Why write it down?"

"That's a question I can't answer. Mysterio was a man who knew what he wanted." Her eyebrows shot to peaks. "Plus he knew where to find me. He didn't need a reminder."

"His cape murdered him," I blurted out.

Both heads swiveled to me.

I cleared my throat as dots of heat popped on my cheeks. "What I mean is, you make clothing that can do things. His cape took control and killed him. We found a sheet of paper with your address ripped off. You say you didn't mind him having other girlfriends, but is that true? Seems to me you could've empowered the cape to kill him in a jealous rage."

Gretchen smiled. "First of all, Mysterio's cape was made years ago and not by me. My power works on clothing that I created, not on someone else's work. Everyone has limitations with their magic. That's mine."

That was awfully convenient for her.

"Let me show you something."

Gretchen walked to the rear of the store. We followed.

"Way to play bad cop," Axel said.

"I want to know what my mother said. That's what this is all about. I don't care about anything else."

He placed a hand on my back. Warmth radiated into my flesh and I immediately felt comfortable, safe. But I reminded myself I'd only known him a few weeks, and his past and his PI experience made him unlike anyone else I'd ever known.

Gretchen flipped a switch, illuminating a storage room. Boxes of all shapes and sizes lined the walls.

"Mysterio's been coming to Magnolia Cove for years. We've been meeting ever since the beginning. He couldn't be mine. I accepted that years ago, and never questioned it. But someone else might not've."

She pressed a shoebox into my hands. I lifted the lid and found letters bound in rubber bands. Dozens of them. "What're these?"

Gretchen folded her arms. "Mysterio lived in his van most of the time. See, he needed places to store things—items that he couldn't keep with him. Told me he wouldn't have saved these, but he felt compelled to for some reason."

Axel picked up one of the banded envelopes and slipped a paper out. "Love letters?"

Gretchen nodded. "Hundreds of them, if not thousands."

I riffled through the stack. "From who? You?"

Gretchen barked a laugh. "You're kidding, right? I don't write love letters to men. Men write them to me."

Well someone thought highly of themselves, didn't they?

"Okay," I said slowly. "So who are they from?"

The bell from the front tinkled. Gretchen grabbed the box and set it with the others. She whirled past us and flipped off the light. "Come."

She reached the front, with me quick on her heels. "Welcome. Let me know if I can help you with anything."

I rounded the corner and saw Cordelia nosing about the shop. My cousin waved dismissively. "Thanks, Gretchen. I'm just looking. I'll let you know if I need anything."

I smiled at Cordelia, who flashed me a quick nod. Then she returned to poking her nose in the jewelry. That was weird. It surprised me that she didn't give more of an acknowledgment.

Gretchen turned toward us. "But anyway, Mysterio had me keep the thousand or so letters."

"Why?" I said. "Since they were *for* him and weren't *from* you."

Gretchen pinched her fingers on a shirt collar and rubbed the fabric. "You think it's odd that a current lover would be holding onto letters from another lover?"

Axel rubbed his neck. "You could say that."

Gretchen smirked. "Thing is, they weren't from a lover."

I clicked my tongue. "What do you mean?"

Gretchen lowered her voice. "They were from someone who wanted to be Mysterio's woman, but wasn't."

It took a moment for dawn to crack in my brain. "You're saying this was unrequited love?"

"Exactly."

"Then why keep the letters?"

"In case something like *this* ever happened." Gretchen leaned in. The faint smell of her rose perfume trickled up my nostrils. "In case Mysterio ever died mysteriously, he wanted proof that there could have been foul play."

"So he had a stalker?" Axel said.

Gretchen shrugged. "I'm not sure if you would call her a stalker, but the relationship didn't go two ways. It was a one way street with her pushing feelings on Mysterio that he didn't return."

"Have you shown these letters to the police?" Axel said.

The bell above the door tinkled again. In strode all six-foot-five of Garrick Young. His gaze swept the store, landing briefly on Cordelia, whose eyes flickered away as if Garrick was on fire.

"Ma'am," Garrick said.

Cordelia whispered a greeting.

His eyes swiveled to us. "Axel, you here about Mysterio's murder?"

Axel rocked on his heels. "Now friend, what would make you ask that?"

Garrick nodded at me. "'Cause that girlfriend of yours likes to solve murders."

I fisted my hands on my hips and said, "As a matter of fact, I'm trying to figure out what message my deceased mother may have given Mysterio. I believe there may be clues in his van. Is it open for me to comb over?"

Garrick shook his head. "Not yet and nice to see your dragon again."

Hugo yawned. I stroked his head. "Thanks. We're bonding."

"Miss Gargoyle, may I speak with you?"

Gretchen walked away and like that, our clue was gone. She'd been whisked off by Garrick, who would find out all about those love letters.

I pulled Axel aside. "Do you think the person who wrote those love letters is who we're looking for? Maybe she found out about Gretchen, wrote the address and then tore the page?"

Axel scrubbed a hand over his face. "You're assuming a couple of things. One is that the person entered Mysterio's room. If this is someone he was leery of, the magician wouldn't have let them in."

"Mm. That's true. But Gretchen has a point. There wasn't any reason for Mysterio to write down her address. He knew it."

"True. Okay, so let's say hypothetically someone did enter Mysterio's room."

"Maybe he wasn't there, they found something with Gretchen's address and wrote it. The problem, though, is that Gretchen didn't say she'd been visited by anyone."

Axel lowered his voice. "Maybe the killer didn't need to. Clearly, it wasn't her they were after—it was Mysterio. He's the one who paid the ultimate price."

"Good point."

Garrick had Gretchen in back. Axel steered me toward the front. "Looks like Gretchen's going to be busy for a while. What do you say we get out of here?"

I stroked Hugo. "But what about the letters? We don't know who wrote them."

Axel was silent as we exited the store and walked toward his truck. He opened my door. I peeled Hugo off me and slipped inside, setting the dragon on my lap.

I rubbed between his eyes. "It's a good thing you don't weigh much. Otherwise, I'd have a headache."

Axel slid in and cranked the engine to purring. He backed up and nosed down the road.

"Okay. You're too quiet. What are we supposed to do now? Garrick's going to know who wrote those letters and we won't."

Axel's lips curled into a coy smile. "Oh, but we do."

My heart accelerated, thundering against my chest. "We do? Who? Who wrote them?"

"Guess."

"Betty Craple."

He barked out a laugh. "No, but almost as good."

I rolled my eyes. "Okay. You going to tell me this century who it is?"

Axel tucked a long strand of dark hair behind his ear. "Idie Claire Hawker."

My jaw dropped. "How'd you figure that out?"

"I peeked."

It was my turn to laugh. "That's awesome. And weird. I would never expect Idie Claire to be an obsessed person."

Axel cocked a brow. "She's a huge gossip."

"Not the same thing." I cracked my knuckles. "Okay. So maybe she stole the paper. But the thing is, Idie's not going to be at her salon for a couple of days. She'll be closed tomorrow and I don't know where she lives."

Axel tipped his face toward me. "If I tell you that I know exactly where to find Idie Claire on a Saturday night, will you kiss me?"

I giggled. "Yes. A small peck on the cheek."

"Oh, then I don't know where she is."

I fisted my hands and pressed them into my thighs. "Okay. I'll kiss you on the mouth."

"Better."

"So where is it? Where does she hang out on Saturday nights?"

He smiled. "At the senior center. Every Saturday Idie's there."

"You're kidding. Why?"

Axel smiled. "Why, she goes dancing, of course."

I cocked a brow. "And I guess that means we're going dancing, too?"

"You got it. Put on your dancing shoes, because we're about to heat up the senior center."

Sounded like a plan. And anything that put Axel's arms around me was even better.

TEN

$\mathcal{W}$e returned to the house, where I unloaded Hugo, putting him in his cage. The dragon blinked at me several times.

"Mama stay."

Awe. My heart pinged at the request. I never thought I'd say it, y'all, but the little ferocious carnivorous dragon was growing on me.

Slowly.

But surely.

But what would happen when he grew to his full size? Which was what? About as big as Betty's house? I couldn't exactly keep him in a house forever. Hugo would become too large. That was simply the reality of the situation.

I crossed to his cage and knelt. I slipped my fingers through the steel squares and said, "Mama will come home soon. Get some rest. I have the feeling Barry the Dragon Tamer is going to have a lot more work for us to do in the morning."

Hugo yawned and curled into a ball. By the time I'd crossed the threshold of my room, I could already hear him snoring.

"You still owe me a kiss," Axel said when I slid into the truck.

I buckled my seatbelt as I laughed. "You'll get your kiss, mister.

Don't worry about it."

He took my hand and brushed it against his lips. "I look forward to it when it happens."

I cleared my throat, hoping it would stop the heat blazing in my nether regions. Whew. Axel sure knew how to steam up a cabin.

"So. Anyway. There's a senior center in Magnolia Cove?"

He dragged his gaze from me back to the road. "It's pretty serious stuff. They have wand classes to keep them current on magical practices, Bingo night and checkers, where they use their familiars instead of actual pieces."

"That's hysterical. How do you know all this?"

"I volunteer there."

I did a double take. "Are you kidding?"

"No. Seniors need to know we're around, Pepper. They need interaction with younger folk. Besides, you never know what sort of nuggets of information you'll learn. Like once I was stuck on a summoning spell. I wasn't going to work a summons, but I needed information on the spell. Unlocking the inner workings was the key to determining who had murdered a young woman. I was frustrated because I couldn't figure it out. I came to the senior center and mentioned it to one of the older residents. He happened to know the answer, which led to an arrest."

I sank into the seat. "Wow. That's cool—the things I learn about you every day. That's pretty awesome about the senior center."

"Don't take the elderly for granted. Without them, we wouldn't be alive. We need their knowledge."

"This conversation suddenly got deep."

Axel chuckled. It was a vast sound that nearly vibrated the cabin. "We're here."

He stopped in front of an ordinary looking ranch style gingerbread cottage. All the structures in Magnolia Cove looked old-world European style and this one was no different. It was white with cream-colored bars crossing it. Floodlights lit the center and illuminated a sign that read MAGNOLIA COVE FIRST WITCH CENTER.

"First witch? What's that mean?"

Axel killed the engine. "That's what a lot of communities call elder witches. First witch. They like the name a lot better than retirement community or senior housing."

I clicked my tongue. "Can't say I blame them."

Axel took my hand as we ascended the steps. "The dance party is off to the right."

I followed him to where music was drifting through the walls. Loud music, I realized.

And not the soft kind.

Hard rock blared through speakers situated inside a room filled with strobe lights, walkers with tennis balls attached on bottom, and geriatrics gyrating to Def Leppard.

No, I'm not kidding.

"Where's the Buddy Holly? Elvis?" I shouted at Axel.

He shook his head. "They're more hip here."

"Don't you mean they're more hip *replacement?*"

He laughed. "Just wait until they do Rage Against the Machine. It's awesome."

What looked like an eighty-year-old woman jiggled right on by. "Come on, youngsters! Get out there on the dance floor! Don't worry; you're too long to break something!"

"Myrtle, I need a dance partner," an old man pushing a walker called out.

I grabbed Axel's arm. "Holy shrimp and grits. This is crazy."

He laughed. "Want to dance?"

I smirked. "Maybe when something quieter comes on?"

He nodded. "Sounds like a plan." He gestured toward the punch table. "I'll go get us a drink."

"It's not spiked is it?"

He chuckled. "It probably is."

Someone's grandmother floated by, her hands high in the air. She wore black jeans, a slashed t-shirt and chains hanging from her belt.

Oh geez. What had I gotten myself into? "If the punch isn't spiked, can you spike it for me?"

Axel winked. "You can count on me."

69

He sauntered off as my gaze floated around the room. Was he sure Idie Claire came here every Saturday? Sure it was rowdy, but it wasn't my idea of a good time.

Then I saw her. Idie stood on the other side of the room behind a wheelchair. A man who looked well into his eighties or even nineties sat in a three-piece suit, a blanket draped over his knees.

Her boyfriend, maybe?

Surely not.

I sneaked a glance at Axel, who had been surrounded by a group of older women. Who could blame them? His dark tresses were pulled back, but his t-shirt revealed bulging arms and his thighs were nearly about to burst through his tight jeans.

The man was built.

There was a reason the ladies in town nicknamed him Mr. Sexy. Because he was.

Realizing the women weren't going to release Axel from their conversation anytime soon, I slipped toward Idie Claire.

A short woman with big boobs cut me off.

"Betty," I said, surprised. "What're you doing here?"

She fisted her hands on her hips. "I like heavy metal. Always have."

Well, that explains it.

"Is it all heavy metal?" I screamed.

"No. They throw a little Kanye in there sometimes, too."

"This is like a hidden gem," I said sarcastically.

Betty nodded. "Tell me about it. I brought Barry. He wanted to come." Her eyebrows wiggled with mischief.

"Barry?" I said.

Betty shot me a secret smile.

I leaned over until I was nearly nose-to-nose with her. "Are you and Barry?" I didn't even know how to ask. Were she and Barry an item?

Barry stood close to Axel at the punch bowls. Blue and pink haired women with dentures shoved in their mouths and thick-lensed glasses swarmed the Dragon Tamer.

Not how I expected to be spending a Saturday night.

"Barry and I aren't your business," Betty snapped. "He's here to help you with the dragon. That's all. I'm just an old woman. My time of love is over."

I frowned. "I love you."

"I know. But that's not the kind of love I'm talking about. Barry and I are just friends. Now, if he was eighty with a pacemaker and a million bucks in the bank, I'd be sitting on his lap."

A laugh choked from my throat.

"But as it is," she continued, "Barry and I are friends. That's it."

"Okay." I pointed over to Idie Claire and the older man she stood behind. "I need to talk to Idie. Can you help with that?"

"I'll take care of the old guy for you. Don't you worry."

The way she said it made a fissure of anxiety weave along my spine. "You're not going to hurt him, are you?"

"Heavens, no. I'll push him wherever he needs to go."

I flattened a hand to my chest. "Oh, okay. That's better."

We threaded through the crowd while Mötley Crüe blared through the speakers. We found Idie, who saw me and flashed a huge smile.

"Pepper Dunn, I didn't expect to see you here."

I never expected to be in this nightmare. "You're a surprise, too. Having fun?"

Idie patted the older man's shoulder. "I come every week to see Grandpa."

The old man held out a hand and we shook. "How do you do? I'm Pepper Dunn."

"Pleasure to meet you," he said. He opened his mouth as if to give his name but stopped.

Idie smiled sadly. She whispered, "He forgets it sometimes."

I realized she meant his name and I gave her a comforting squeeze on the shoulder.

"Yeah, I came because Betty told me all about this place. Said it's a ton of fun."

Betty bobbed her head to the music.

Idie elbowed me. "Hey, didn't I see you at Mysterio's show the other night?"

Bingo! I didn't even have to force my way in. "Yep, I was there."

Idie's eyes misted. "Wasn't he wonderful? Connecting people with their lost loved ones is truly a talent."

"Some people think he's a phony," I yelled as the music kicked into higher gear.

Idie shook her head. "He wasn't fake. I went every year and always had a loved one visit me. Always. They might not've looked the way I remembered, but they came. In fact, my dad did hide something behind the toilet, just like Mysterio said."

Oh, I had to know the answer to this. "What?"

"Under a loose tile, there was old witch money. Several hundred years ago, witches used it instead of the dollar. Eventually, they converted to American currency, but it took a while. The money's not worth much, but it was important to him." She fluffed her hair and said, "Didn't someone come through for you?"

I knuckled away a tear threatening to slide down my cheek. "My mom."

"She had a message, right? Something private?"

The time was ripe. "It's funny you should ask. Mysterio died before he could give it to me. I found a slip of paper I thought had the message on it, but it was partly destroyed. I've been trying to figure out if someone has the rest of the page—possibly someone who saw Mysterio right before he died." I wiggled my brows at her. "Someone close to him. Weren't y'all close?"

Idie bit her lip. "We...kept in contact the months when he wasn't here. I think that's why so many of my kin showed up for his shows." Her jaw flexed. "You see, Mysterio and I were linked in a strange way."

Okay.

How to put this delicately?

"Oh? It's so funny you say that, because I came across hundreds of love letters written by you to Mysterio."

Her jaw dropped.

Okay, so I wasn't subtle or delicate. I didn't have time for that crap anyway. I needed to know what my mother wanted to tell me. Every second counted because the longer Mysterio was dead, the less likely it would be that I would discover the truth.

At least, that's what I figured. Besides, no one was saying the opposite, so it must be true.

Idie grabbed my hand.

"Will you watch her grandpa?" I said to Betty, who pulled out her corncob pipe in response. I took that as a yes.

Idie dragged me outside. The music waned and the sound of frogs and crickets filled the honeysuckle-sweet air.

I blinked when I noticed the fire blazing in Idie's eyes. "What are you talking about, love letters?"

Suddenly I wanted to disappear. But instead, I crossed my arms. "I have it on good authority that you've been sending Mysterio love letters for years. And not just one or two. I'm talking hundreds."

She covered her face and moaned.

I dug in. "Someone was in Mysterio's room before he died. They tore off a sheet of paper that had an address on it. That paper may hold the secret of what my mother wanted me to know. Idie, was it you? Did you take the paper?"

She moaned again.

"Did you discover that Mysterio had other lovers and decide to get rid of him? Is that what happened?"

She raked her fingers through her hair and sniffled. "No. It wasn't me. I didn't have anything to do with Mysterio's death, and I wasn't in his room. I don't know anything about the sheet of paper."

I folded my arms. "Unrequited love can lead to jealousy and that jealousy can often lead to murder."

Idie shook her head. "You don't understand. Those letters weren't from me."

I cocked a brow in disbelief. "They had your name all over them. So if they weren't from you, who wrote them?"

Idie pursed her lips. "They weren't from me. They were from Mysterio's dead wife."

I blinked. "What?"

Idie smiled. "I'm a medium. Spirits sometimes speak through me."

ELEVEN

*T*here was a swing set outside the senior center. Apparently the geriatrics enjoyed settling into a kid's swing and gliding back and forth.

Turned out, so did I.

"But that doesn't make any sense," I said to Idie Claire. "If you're a medium, why would you go to Mysterio's show once a year to see your kin?"

Idie gripped the chains before pushing off. "Lots of spirits come through to me. Unfortunately, it's folks I'm not related to. No blood kin. With so many ghosts appearing, I wondered if my relatives would visit another medium. That's how I started attending Mysterio's shows. At first, I'd heard the rumors that he was a phony. I didn't know what to think, but one year I figured I'd give it a shot. See if he was made of cheese and crackers like I thought he might be, or if he full of sourdough, like others said."

"What?"

Idie smiled. "I make up funny phrases sometimes. Anyway, the first show I attended, my dead brother showed up. Right there in the middle of the stage. I was floored. He'd died when a spell he was working went bad and killed him. I'd always wondered what happened. I tried several times to contact him, but my calls went unanswered."

She gazed into the starry sky and inhaled deeply. "But there he stood beside Mysterio. From that moment I knew Mysterio was no phony. Not in the least. But that's also when it started."

"What?" I said, digging my toes in the soft sand beneath me.

"Mysterio's dead wife visited me that very night. I was terrified. I didn't know who this lady was, and she was flooding my brain with all sorts of images and thoughts about Mysterio. When I finally calmed her, she pushed me to grab pen and paper. That's when I started writing the love letters—her love letters to him. That first night, I must've written for two hours straight. My hand had a cramp the likes of which you'd never believe." A throaty laugh escaped Idie's lips. "Human emotions are so complicated. They're never cut and dry, and Heather's weren't either."

"That was his wife?"

She nodded. "A lot of hurt happened between those two. She needed to purge it. I figured Mysterio must've been a lot like me—his dead relatives maybe couldn't visit him, either. The next day I tracked Mysterio down, gave him the letter. He said he didn't want anything to do with his dead wife."

"Why not?"

"At first I didn't understand it, either. But Heather continued to visit me. I managed to get hold of an address for Mysterio and sent the letters. It didn't matter whether or not he wanted them. This woman had a lot to say. The least he could do was read what she had me write."

Idie paused. "Most of the time Heather talked about how much she loved him. But then the letters became different. Apparently, they'd fought a lot before she died. She knew he was cheating on her and boy, did she have a lot to say about him stepping out on her."

The wind picked up. Idie sniffed. "Do you smell that?"

"What?" I said.

"Gardenias." Her gaze swept the grounds. "I don't see any, though."

The breeze kicked a soft tendril of hair into my mouth. I smoothed it away. "So is that all? For years you wrote Mysterio letters from a dead wife?"

Idie confirmed it. "That's it. I wrote letters. I explained that even though he didn't want them, I felt compelled to send them. I would sign my own name, but also put Heather's name on the page as well. Mysterio said he understood, but I doubt he ever read any." She slanted her head toward me. "How'd you find out about them, anyway?"

"Mysterio gave them to Gretchen Gargoyle to hold. She seems to think that you were obsessed with him."

Idie barked a laugh. "It's not me who was obsessed. Read one. You'll see."

I pushed off, sailing on the swing. "I believe they weren't from you. But did Heather ever talk about wanting revenge?"

If Heather could contact Idie and have her write, what else could she have done from the spirit world?

Idie shook her head. "No. She was sad and angry, but Heather never wanted to hurt her husband. You know, I'm not the only person who followed Mysterio and attended his show whenever he came to town. You should also talk to Hattie Hollypop. She owns Brews and Jewels."

I pushed out of the swing. "They're probably closed tomorrow."

Idie smiled. "They are, but I overheard someone say—in fact, it was Gretchen. Gretchen Gargoyle mentioned that Hattie attends morning witch's yoga in the park every Sunday. I know for a fact."

"Gretchen mentioned it?"

"I did her hair today."

My eyes lit up. "Thanks for the tip."

Idie glanced at my tresses. "Don't forget. Come in anytime to get a cut. And you know what, Pepper? First cut's on me. I have an opening Tuesday."

"I'll think about it."

As Idie climbed toward the senior center, Axel strode down the knoll. I started toward him.

"Had all the swinging you can take?"

I smiled. "I could continue. Care to join me?"

"Don't mind if I do."

We sat next to each other. The chains creaked and groaned as we drifted back and forth. "So what'd you find out?"

"You might already know, but Idie's a medium. The letters are from Mysterio's dead wife."

He scrubbed a hand over his cheek. "Interesting."

"Idie doesn't claim to know anything and she doesn't strike me as the type to murder."

"You'd be surprised," he said in a low, Southern drawl that made a shiver race along my spine.

"I could totally be wrong, but I don't think so."

He cocked a brow. "Oh? And why, Pepper Dunn, do you believe so fiercely that Idie Claire Hawker is not the type to murder?"

"Why do I get the feeling you're not talking about Idie anymore?"

His expression darkened. Axel tapped his fingers on the chain. "'Cause I'm not."

"What are you talking about?"

Axel's harsh gaze sent a spear straight to my heart. I shuddered. "Sometimes even the people closest to you can betray, Pepper."

I glanced left and right. "Have I missed something?"

He laughed, which lightened the mood by about a thousand degrees. "No, you haven't missed anything. It's something I haven't told you, but it looks like it's time. I'm talking about my brother."

"Oh." I pressed a finger between my eyes, smoothing out the worry wrinkle that had bloomed.

There was so much I still didn't know about the mysterious Axel. Yes, he was a werewolf. And yes, he had been accused of killing some witch's sheep, and that's how he ended up in Magnolia Cove—because he had been on the run from them when he arrived. And his parents were living out of an RV in the Rockies. But this, this was news.

"You have a brother."

"Oh, do I ever have a brother. Guy's been in and out of trouble for a while. He was a good kid growing up. The best. Great guy. But then something happened. He got in with the wrong crowd. They put dark notions in his head. None of us—my parents and me—knew until it was too late."

I rose and crossed to stand in front of Axel. He took my hands and pulled me to him. I eased onto his lap. It was awkward, sitting on him while he sat in a swing, but somehow we made the whole balancing thing work.

He had pulled his hair out of its holder and it hung loosely over his shoulders. I ran my fingers through his thick dark locks.

"Showing off your hair to the ladies?"

He chuckled, revealing a perfect smile. "No. One of them yanked it out when I wasn't looking. Those ladies are gropers. You gotta watch them."

I laughed. Silence lay pregnant between us. I felt the weight of the conversation and shifted it to his brother. "So none of you knew *what* until it was too late?"

Axel's head fell against one chain. "My brother let the wild of the werewolf take hold of him in his human form. He would play on the feral aspect, letting the testosterone rule his body. He became violent. He'd start bar fights, attack people for no reason. It got to the point where he became uncontrollable. The scales tipped and my brother did the unthinkable."

Axel paused, sucked in air. His gaze drifted up to mine. He stroked my hair and pulled me down for a kiss that made my toes curl.

We parted and I inhaled the sweet air. "Why do I get the feeling you're trying to distract me?"

He chuckled. "Is it so bad I want a kiss?"

"Nope. Not bad at all." I traced my fingers along his jaw. His stubble pricked my skin and reminded me that beneath his cool exterior lay a rough, wild beast—one that was contained, but a beast nonetheless.

For a flicker of a moment, I wondered exactly how safe I was?

But the thought vanished as quickly as it had bloomed.

He sighed. "My brother started selling—things he shouldn't have. Rare, exotic items that are illegal."

"Like what?"

His jaw flexed. "Illegal potions, that sort of thing. Eventually, he got caught dealing large volumes and was sent away for three years.

"By the time he went to prison, I no longer recognized him. A man who only a few months earlier had been kind was now completely changed. He wasn't the brother I knew any longer. He was someone else."

I slid off Axel's lap and sat on the other swing, facing in his direction. "Axel, I'm not questioning who you are. I hope I didn't say something to make you think that."

He rubbed his thumb over an eyebrow. "No, it's not that. What you said about Idie reminded me of him. Of what my brother could've been, compared to what he is."

"You know," I said, "if I'd stayed in Nashville, I would be living on the streets. There's another comparison for you. Less than a month ago I had no focus, no future. Heck, I was a waitress at an animal-themed restaurant. Maybe a little distance from bad influences can go a long way."

He scowled. "It can."

"Come on, Axel. There's something you're not telling me. I'm all fine and good with some secrets. Heck, I don't expect you to tell me everything about yourself in one day. I don't want to run away screaming, after all."

He laughed. "I know. And if you start calling me every five minutes, that would kill my buzz for you, too."

I grinned. "Don't worry. I erase your phone number every time you call just so I won't be tempted."

"Good thing." He launched into a long swing before coming to rest next to me. "My brother's been in prison. Served two years."

"And?"

"And I got a message earlier from a contact in law enforcement.

"About?"

Axel's lips twitched as if he wanted to blurt out what clearly had knotted his tongue. His gaze swept from me to the stars and toward the senior center.

"My brother and I—"

"—Does he have a name?" I interrupted.

"Adam."

I clicked my tongue. "Adam. Got it. Recorded in my memory. What about Adam?"

"We haven't gotten along since he started to change."

"Okay. Well, you know, I've got issues with guys, too. Rufus attacks me hoping to steal my head witch power, or whatever he wants. Join the club. I get it."

Axel shook his head. "It's more than that. Adam tried to make me feral with him. He wanted me to be part of his little thing. He went so far as to try to get me to smoke, thought it would influence me his way. I wouldn't do any of it, of course. That wasn't for me. That's another reason that why when the witches up north thought I'd been killing livestock—why that knife twisted in my gut so hard. It was an old wound. Adam wanted me to be one way. I wanted to be another."

I frowned. "So what's so important about all this now?"

He scraped the heel of his hand over his chin. "The message I received about Adam—he escaped from prison."

My heart thundered. "Where do you think he'd go?"

Axel's gaze made me freeze in my swing. "We used to be close, the two of us. He might want that connection again. If he knows where I am, there's one place he'd go."

I swallowed. "You mean here? Magnolia Cove?"

His fingers tightened on the chain until his knuckles paled. "You got it."

TWELVE

"*B*ut what about the police? Do they know? Are they searching for him?" I said, feeling a surge of panic scramble up my throat.

Axel gazed at the ground. "They know. A lot of folks are looking for him, but Adam is resourceful. He's good at evading authorities when he needs to."

"But he can't just hide in plain sight," I said.

Axel lifted his face to me. His expression was a contortion of pain that made my knees shake. "Pepper, he can be dangerous. Right now, I need to focus on taking care of that part of my life."

"Okay," I said, trying to sound chipper. "If you need to focus on that, that's what you have to do."

"I don't think you understand."

"What?"

"I think we should cool off for a while."

I swallowed a knot of emotion in the back of my throat. "You want to break up? Over this?"

He exhaled a shot of air. "I can't focus on you and my brother. It wouldn't be fair to you. I'll still be your friend and help however I can with tracking down the information your mother left Mysterio, but that's all I can give right now."

I shifted my gaze to the soft ground beneath me. "I'm not asking you to give more," I said quietly.

"I know."

"But this is your decision?"

"It is."

I tried not to be angry. I really did, but I still felt a swell of pain rumble in my chest.

That was stupid. Axel and I barely knew each other. We'd only been dating a week, I couldn't be all torn up about him cooling his jets.

Could I?

Whatever. I didn't need a boyfriend anyway. I could be friends with Axel. No problem. I could do it.

Even if it did feel like someone had taken a hot poker and rammed it into my heart.

I was a big girl and wore big girl panties. If he just wanted to be friends, I could do that.

Besides, I didn't want to be with a guy whose brother wanted to influence him in bad ways anyhow.

But then why did it hurt so much?

"Okay," I said. "I understand."

The drive to Betty's house was quiet. There was nothing to say. Nothing would turn back the clock and mend us together, and nothing he could say would ease the throb of pain in my heart.

His lips brushed my cheek as we stood on the front porch. "I'll talk to you soon," he said.

I plastered on a huge, supportive grin. I would not let him know how much he'd hurt me. "Okay. Let me know if I can help."

He brought his hands to his heart. "That's why I like you so much. Always thinking of others."

Then why'd you break up with me?

We said goodnight. A row of buds dipped down to sniff me. I patted Jennie, the guard-vine. "Sleep tight," I whispered.

As much as I wanted to eat about a dozen ice cream sundaes and wallow in a pity party, I pushed my feelings to the side and decided to stay busy. That was what I needed.

I also figured it would be best not to mention any of this to my family—at least not yet.

If I talked about it, I would start crying and I really, really didn't want to cry.

Not because I didn't care about Axel, but because I did. I didn't understand how I could care about him so quickly and so fully.

Basically, I didn't want to admit that he'd wrecked me because I was stronger than that.

The next morning, I was dressed and ready for some early morning yoga. I had on yoga pants, a yoga shirt and I even wore what I considered to be the perfect yoga headband. It was black, kept my hair out of my face and didn't pinch my noggin too tightly.

My eyes grazed over the spread of grits, country ham, skillet hash browns, biscuits and gravy. I grabbed an apple from a bowl.

"Sorry. I've got to skip breakfast. I've got morning yoga today."

Betty squinted at me so hard her bottom lip nearly touched her nose. "You going to that baloney?"

I bit into the apple and spoke between chews. "Yes, because that baloney might help me figure out what it was my mom wanted me to know."

"She wanted you to know that she loves you," Betty said.

"That's not what I mean. What she told Mysterio."

"I know what you mean."

Cordelia poured a cup of coffee from a carafe at the sidebar and yawned. "As much fun as crack-of-butt—I mean crack-of-dawn, yoga sounds, I'm afraid that's more exercise than I can handle this early in the morning."

"Late date night?" I chirped.

Cordelia flashed me a sour look. "I have no idea what you're talking about."

Betty's gaze zipped from me to Cordelia. She opened her mouth to speak when Amelia bounded down the stairs.

"Ooh! So you're going to the Sunday morning yoga class? The one at the meadow behind the courthouse?"

"That's the one."

Amelia plopped into a chair and started heaving gobs of food onto an empty plate. "I hear it's a lot of fun. You'll have a good time. I'd love to join you but I'm allergic to yoga. All those positions make me hurt just looking at them."

I cringed. Wow. I hadn't bothered to think about the positions. How was I going to pretzel my body into some of those contortions? Maybe I could just sit those out.

"The instructor makes everyone go into the positions," Amelia said, "whether you're a newbie or not."

So much for my hope of not looking like a complete idiot. "Well, I guess I need to be on my way. I've got about ten minutes before it starts."

Amelia scrunched up her eyebrows. "What about Hugo?"

"What about him?"

"Aren't you taking him?"

I sank onto one hip. "Now why would I take a dragon with me to yoga class?"

Cordelia finished a sip of coffee. "Because it's a *familiar* yoga class. You're supposed to bring your pet familiar. Helps you bond. It's like doing yoga with your baby."

"I've never heard of doing yoga with a baby."

Cordelia flipped her golden hair over one shoulder. "I'm sure someone does it somewhere."

"That doesn't sound like a thing,"

Amelia smiled brightly. "But familiar yoga is. You'll have to take Hugo or they won't let you into the class."

Great. "Okay. Well, everyone cross your fingers that he doesn't spew fire on the instructor."

Betty swiped a napkin across her mouth. "I'm betting he does."

"Thank you. That helps me feel better," I said sarcastically.

"You're welcome."

~

WHEN I ARRIVED at the class I felt like a total idiot. There were about ten other witches all with their regular, normal familiars. Most of them were cats, though I did see a couple of dogs.

And none of them had a dragon—much less a baby one named Hugo.

I glanced around, looking for Hattie Hollypop, but didn't see her. What I did see were witches keeping a wide berth from me. A couple of cats hissed and a dog growled.

"He's only a baby," I said to the animals. "He's not going to hurt anybody."

"I'll scratch his eyes out if he tries," said one particularly feisty Siamese cat.

I dodged the animals and worked my way to the back of the crowd. At least that way, if Hattie happened to show up late, maybe I could work my way up to her.

Gretchen Gargoyle arrived. I realized she must've known about Hattie coming to the class because she came herself. She took a spot off to the side.

The instructor, a tall extra thin redhead with long arms and slim legs, came to the front and put her hands together. She gave us all a wide smile.

"A big welcome to all the witches I've seen before and to those of you who are new." She tipped her body to the left and looked squarely at me. "I see at least one new member in our little yoga coven. Do your best to follow along. I will come and correct you. Be sure to breathe deeply and enjoy this time to connect with your familiar. I see we have a new animal—a dragon. How exciting. I hope he won't try to eat any of the other creatures."

She blinked at me as if expecting an answer.

"No," I said quickly. "He won't eat anyone."

I didn't think.

"How wonderful," she continued. "Now. Let's get started, shall we?

Everyone cradle your animals in front of you like so, and extend your left leg back."

The instructor held a small hedgehog in her arms while demonstrating the pose. "She's got a tiny animal, and I've got you," I said to Hugo.

"Mama," he said.

I was in mid-leg extension when a woman with blond hair huffed toward me. She wore a sour expression and her boobs were barely contained by her yoga clothes.

"This spot taken?" she said.

It took me a couple of blinks, but I realized it was Hattie Hollypop. Whoa. Did she look different on a Sunday morning than when I'd last seen her strolling with Mysterio.

When she'd been with Mysterio, Hattie had been dolled up with makeup and her hair slicked up into a ponytail.

Now she was frizz city with a hair that looked more like what a cat coughed up than the Brazilian Blowout look she'd had before.

Just saying.

She gestured with her palms out as if waiting for my response. "Is this spot taken?" she asked again.

"What? Oh, no. Sorry. I've got Sunday morning brain. It's like a fog in my head."

She slinked in beside me. "Join the club."

Hattie pulled a cat from a bag and held it in her arms. It was a plain looking red tabby. The animal glanced at me and then at Hugo.

"Good morning," the cat said.

"Morning," I murmured. I smiled at Hattie. "Your cat said hello."

Hattie's gaze slid toward me. "You must be the new familiar matcher."

"I am." I extended my hand. "Pepper Dunn."

"Hattie Hollypop." She raised the cat. "This is Joe. He loved going to the familiar shop when Donovan owned it."

"That was my great-uncle."

Hattie gave Joe a good scratch. "Yeah, he and Donovan were big old buddies. Isn't that right, Joe?"

Joe stared at Hugo. "I see you have the dragon."

"You know about him?" I said with surprise.

"Oh yes," Joe said in a bored voice. "Your uncle told me he'd ordered him. Wanted it to be a surprise for his niece."

I leaned over. "So it's true. I wasn't sure as Donovan didn't leave a note."

We were interrupted by the instructor. "I hear some talking. Less talking and more practice, ladies. We're all here to bond with our familiars. Get closer to them so we can work the best magic possible."

She eyed me like I was grounded for the week.

"She's so serious," Hattie said. "Nina's nothing if not in control."

I stretched Hugo out in front of me. "Her name's Nina?"

Hattie nodded. "She works in the magical objects store. Takes this yoga stuff seriously."

"Well, we're all here, aren't we? I guess we must take it seriously, too."

Nina's clipped voice grabbed my attention. "Now, using your magic, suspend your familiars in the air in front of you while you connect with them."

Say what?

I was actually supposed to do magic? Crap. That wasn't my strongest suit.

With my gaze steady on Hugo, I lifted him out in front of me. The innocence in his eyes made my heart cinch. Emotions tugged at me and I felt the need to be his protector, to coddle and make sure this little dragon stayed safe and sound.

I extended him outward and focused on levitating the dragon. I concentrated, pinpointing my energy into that singular thought. I watched as the other witches released their familiars. The animals hovered in the air while their witches moved into tree position.

I pulled one hand away. Hugo started to fall. I snatched him up.

Nina came over. Great. I'd caught the teacher's attention. I felt like such an idiot.

Nina placed her hands on my shoulders. "It can be hard with a new familiar," she whispered in my ear, "but focus on the connection the two of you have."

"What connection?" I blurted out.

"The thing that brought you together in the first place."

"He arrived in a package and hatched."

"Oh. Well, try to find the string holding you together."

I frowned, but I tried to focus on some sort of string. Was it like a magical string? Was it made of yarn or was it really thin like thread?

Yes, these were the thoughts that collided in my head.

"Now look at him. Really see your familiar."

I stared into Hugo's sweet baby face and felt a snap in my core. Something pulled and stretched, harnessing me to him.

A rush of powers flooded my body and at that moment, I knew I could let go.

And I did.

I pulled my hands from Hugo and watched as he hovered in front of me.

Nina patted my shoulder. "See? It's not so hard, is it? Trust and connection. That's all it takes to bring two people together. Trust and the connection will follow."

Yeah, that didn't remind me of Axel at all.

That was sarcasm.

Nina stepped away.

I felt our bond tighten as if the string joining us had thickened or something. It was weird and super cool at the same time.

"He's cute," Hattie whispered. "An adorable baby dragon. You say you got him in a package?"

I nodded. "Yeah. He arrived a few days ago." Here it was. My opening. "I sold him to Mysterio."

She did a double take. "The magician?"

"Oh, did you know him?"

Hattie moved from tree to warrior. I followed, though very wobbly. "Yes. I knew him."

"Right before he died, Mysterio wrote part of a message from my dead mother on a slip of paper. Unfortunately, half of it was ripped off."

We shifted to tree. "I may be able to help you with that."

"How?"

Up front, one of the cats started screeching. It jumped on a terrier that immediately started snarling and biting.

"Cat fight," Hattie said.

Within about two seconds, half the familiars in yoga class had jumped into the fray. Hissing, barking and growling filled the calm Sunday morning.

I met Hugo's gaze and the baby dragon flew straight up into the air.

"Hugo, come back," I yelled, but it was no use. Either he didn't hear me, he ignored me, or he simply didn't understand what I was saying because let's face it—he was only a few days old.

He swooped high into the sky and plummeted down, aiming straight for the tangle of animals.

Hugo opened his mouth and an arrow of flames shot toward the familiars. My heart lurched and my stomach clenched as the line of fire licked toward the dogs and cats.

Fear overtook me. I didn't want any creatures hurt. I threw my emotion toward the animals. It worked. Hugo's flames stopped short as if they hit an invisible wall.

I stared at Hugo as he swept over the familiars. The sound of fire had killed all the fight in them. The dogs and cats parted. They gazed at the dragon, who had swooped past them and was sailing into the sky.

One of the witches pointed a hand at Hugo and yelled, "That dragon tried to kill my doggie. It wanted to kill and eat my dog. Call that new sheriff."

Great. I almost missed aunts Mint and Licky. Even they weren't as much trouble as this.

Or maybe I'm just not remembering their antics as well.

Yep. That's probably it.

THIRTEEN

"So the dragon's already causing problems."

I sat in Garrick Young's office. I sat in a chair with Hugo perched next to me. "He didn't cause the problem, but that's neither here nor there."

Garrick threaded his fingers together and propped his elbows on his desk. "He breathes fire."

I smirked. "Maybe it's like removing scent glands in ferrets. You remove a gland, stop a dragon breathing fire, no one gets hurt."

Garrick chuckled. "I don't think it works that way."

I cocked a brow. "Are you sure?"

"Yes," he said in a sobering tone.

I patted Hugo's head. His tongue lolled from his mouth like a dog's. "It may have seemed like he was about to barbecue those creatures, but he wasn't. I know he wasn't. I could feel it."

Garrick leaned back and stretched his legs out to the side of the desk. "It may have seemed to you like he wasn't going to hurt those animals, but I've got about ten witnesses who say otherwise."

I shrugged. "I don't know what to say. My uncle ordered him before I ever arrived in Magnolia Cove. My grandmother says this little guy is supposed to protect me. He's only a few days old."

"And already scaring the masses."

Someone knocked on the door. Garrick's gaze swiveled from me. "It's open."

A dark head of hair popped in. "I hear there was a ruckus in the park."

My heart fluttered to my throat. Axel.

"Come on in."

Axel shut the door behind him and leaned against it. His gaze flitted to me briefly before settling on Garrick. "I heard the basics. Seems to me there was a bit of hysteria."

"It's a dragon," Garrick said.

Axel crossed his arms. "It's a baby."

"That breathes fire."

"That's what I've been saying," I said quickly. "It breathes fire. People will be afraid of it."

Axel glared at me as if to say whose-side-are-you-on? "It can be trained otherwise. It's young."

Garrick drummed his fingers on the chair's armrests. "I don't need these folks to be in danger. Or even to *feel* like they're in danger from one of the familiars."

"No one was hurt. From what I understand the dragon wasn't going after the witches."

"He wasn't," I added quickly. "Hugo wasn't attacking anyone. He was trying to break up a fight the other animals were having. A cat attacked a dog and then a whole bunch of animals started fighting. If you want to point fingers at an animal, you need to find the cat that started the mess to begin with." I folded my arms defiantly. "I can find the attack kitty if you need me to. I was there. I'm a witness."

A slow smile curled on Garrick's lips. "So according to you, the dragon didn't start the ruckus."

"Right. He was trying to end it."

Garrick's gaze focused on me. "Do you have proof?"

I faltered. "Anyone there can tell you that Hugo didn't singe a hair on anyone. But can they explain what I felt? That Hugo's entire intent

91

was to stop the fight? I can't give you a one hundred percent 'yes' on that."

The officer slowly nodded. "In that case, since no one was hurt, the one thing I can do is give you a warning. Watch the dragon. It's hard to have a familiar like that. They're rare, and folks love them because of their mythology. But people also fear them. You're going to encounter more fear than you are fascination. I could be wrong, though. Could be wrong."

I scooped Hugo into my arms. He squeaked as I hugged him to me. "I'm sorry that he scared folks and I'll do what I can to make sure nothing like that happens again."

Axel flashed me a brief smile. He moved from the door and opened it. "Thanks, Garrick."

Garrick waved him away. "Welcome."

I was nearly out the door when I heard Garrick's voice. "Oh, and Pepper?"

I turned. "Yes?"

"Watch that dragon. I let y'all off this time, but next time may be different."

I felt one corner of my lips tip into a smile. "I understand."

He nodded as Axel shut the door.

A moment later, the private detective was ushering me through the station. He held a warm hand to my spine as we clipped along.

As soon as we were out the door, Axel whispered in my ear. "What happened?"

So I explained it all over again. He looked concerned. "Just what exactly were you doing there in the first place?"

"Idie Claire told me that Hattie might know something about Mysterio. I was trying to get close to her."

"By barbecuing her pet?"

I bristled. "It wasn't her animal that started the fight. Besides, what are you doing here anyway? You wanted to cool things off."

He scowled. "That doesn't mean I can't try to help you."

I growled in frustration. Axel cocked a brow.

"This is what I've been saying all along about Hugo. Dragons are dangerous. But no one wanted to listen to me. Everyone thinks I need to keep the fire-breathing, large animal-eating creature. Keep a dangerous beast as a pet; everything will be fine."

"I never said everything would be fine."

"I'm pretty sure you did."

He chuckled.

I balled up my one free fist—the one that wasn't clutching Hugo to my chest. "This is not funny."

"No, it's not. I agree. Why don't you let me take him?"

"What?"

He shrugged. "It might help cool Garrick along with the rest of the town. I don't have to take him for forever, just long enough to get some heat off you."

I shook my head. "No."

"Think about it."

I raised my chin. "I have. Answer's no."

Axel exhaled deeply. "Your baby dragon scared half the town."

"It wasn't half the town," I said.

"By the time the gossips get ahold of it, it'll be half the town."

I nibbled the inside of my lip. "Hm. Think we can use that in our favor?"

"How?"

I grinned broadly. "No idea. But if you give me enough time I'm sure I can figure something out."

Axel chuckled. "Come on. Want some breakfast?"

I sighed. "Should we really do that? I don't need you screwing with my emotions, Axel."

He winced. "I'm not trying. Just wanted to take you out for breakfast."

Maybe I could have a meal with him and not get my heart raked over burning coals that would turn me into a shriveled mess?

It was worth a shot.

I'd checked the wall clock on the way out of the police station. It was after ten and I was starved. "Lord, yes. Where are we going? It's Sunday morning. What is open this early besides Spellin' Skillet?"

Axel opened the door to his Mustang. I slid inside and looked at him expectantly. "The pop-up restaurant's open."

"Barbecue for breakfast?"

He shook his head. "No. They have a Sunday brunch buffet."

"Are you trying to make me fat? Because it's not going to work. I was chunky in high school and worked hard to shed those pounds. I'll eat a grain of salt for breakfast before I put on weight."

He raised his hands in surrender. "No one's trying to give you complex."

"Good."

We headed over to the pop-up restaurant, where I built a plate with pecan cinnamon rolls and sausage. Axel studied my food while I fed Hugo links from under the table. That was much more my speed than mice.

"You're eyeing my plate," I said, forking a roll.

"Is it making you uncomfortable?"

I glanced up. His blue eyes locked on me. I couldn't pull away. I inhaled sharply and swallowed a knot of food. I choked, coughing into my hand and sucking air like I was drowning.

"No. It's not making me uncomfortable. Want a link?"

Axel cut into a slice of ham. "Even if I wanted it, looks like Hugo might fight me for it."

"He's a lover, not a fighter."

"Right."

Pixie the pixie arrived floating a pitcher of sweet tea beside her. "Y'all need refills?"

"Yes, thanks," I said.

She poured some and I realized I didn't have any jelly beans. Axel pulled a bag from his pocket and laid it on the table. "That what you're missing?"

I sank my forehead onto my hand. "You're really bad at this whole cooling the jets thing."

"I'd bought those last week and forgot to give them to you."

"That almost makes this appropriate." I opened it and found a small collection of colorful beans. "Thank you."

Red dotted his cheeks. "You're welcome."

I plopped a few in and tasted. Fruit flavors swirled with the orange pekoe tea. Perfect. I smacked my lips. "It's wonderful."

"Great, because you've got a lot of work to do."

I frowned. "About what?"

"The dragon. If you don't get him under control, you're going to have this town at your doorstep with pitchforks and torches."

My stomach clenched. "That's a problem."

"I'd say so. You need to work with Barry. See how he can help bond the two of you because if you have another outburst like you had today, I'm afraid Garrick won't have any choice but to take him in."

I glanced at the sweet face. Spikes dotted his eyes and his tongue dipped out one side of his mouth as he patiently waited for another sausage.

"All right. I'll find Barry and have him help train Hugo." Axel stopped chewing. "You don't have to get mad at me. I'm trying to keep you both safe."

I raked my fingers through my hair. "I know. It's a lot, that's all." I inhaled a deep cleansing breath and released it. "But it'll be fine. Baby steps."

He reached across as if he wanted to take my hand, but stopped before he touched me. "Baby steps."

I shot him a feeble smile. We finished up lunch and headed to Betty's house. Axel left me at the curb and I padded up the porch and inside.

I found Betty standing at the dining room table, a huge map of Magnolia Cove hovering about it. She had a long pointy stick in her hand. The sharp end of it was stationed on the park. She looked like a general assigning posts for an upcoming battle.

"General Custer, I assume," I said.

"You're just in time," she said.

"What are you doing? Rounding the troops?" I said.

She fisted her hands on her hips. "I was about to, but then you entered."

I deposited Hugo on the floor and studied her. "Were you in here talking to yourself? It looks like you're going over military plans."

Betty smirked. "These are not military plans."

"What is it then?"

"It's a map putting together the timelines between you receiving the dragon, Mysterio's death, and everything else that's happened so far—including the fiasco at the park this morning."

I sank into a chair and wished I had a shot of bourbon to take the edge off what this Sunday had already done to me. Witches or not, Sunday was still the Lord's day and I was pretty sure drinking was frowned upon in Magnolia Cove.

"You look like you could use a drink," Betty said.

"I'm not going to drink alcohol on a Sunday morning, even if my dragon's been accused of trying to fricassee half the town."

"I heard it was three-quarters."

"Same thing."

A spark glinted in Betty's eyes. "Magnolia Cove is dry on Sundays. You can't buy liquor, but what're they going to do if I've already got some?"

She hummed as she made her way to a cabinet door. She opened it and returned with two tulip-shaped glasses and a flask with a golden liquid inside.

"What's that?"

Betty smiled. "Honeysuckle wine. Only takes a thimble full to knock the edge off. Drink the whole thing and we'll be taking you to the ER for alcohol poisoning."

I narrowed my eyes. "Is that legal?"

"Sort of."

"That doesn't make me feel better."

"That might not, but this will." She poured a teensy bit in the glass and pushed it over. "Drink up. It'll help."

I grimaced, but then decided what the heck? I downed the glass. The small amount of liquid was barely enough to wet my tongue, but about half a minute later, my shoulders drooped, a sloppy smile spread across my face and I heaved a huge sigh as I sank farther into the chair.

"Wow. That is some good stuff."

"Takes the edge off, right?" Betty said, grinning.

"Sure does. That's awesome. Well, where were we?"

Betty paced, the pointy stick clasped behind her. "We were at ground zero, where Mysterio died."

I propped my chin in my palm and leaned forward. "I don't understand why we're there. Why are we at ground zero and why are we talking about Mysterio?"

"Because I'm convinced all of this is linked—you receiving the dragon, Mysterio dying and everything else in between—even the dragon's antics this morning."

"How do you know about that?"

She wiggled her eyebrows. "I have my ways."

I splayed out my hand. "Wait. First of all, you're the person who said that Uncle Donovan ordered the dragon to protect me."

"That's what I thought. At first. But now I see how this plot has thickened and I'm convinced there's more to it than that. Mysterio happened to walk in right after the dragon hatched? He died before returning the creature to you? Then the dragon spits fire into a crowd of creatures?"

"Not to mention the note from my mother."

Betty cleared her throat. "There ain't a note from your mother."

I backed up. "No need to get all redneck on me about it. Mysterio said there was a note. He even started to write it out. There *is* a note."

Betty's head jerked left and right. "Kid, the only thing your mother ever would've wanted you to know is that she loved you with all her heart. To the moon and back, and all that crap."

"That's not a nice thing to say," I mumbled.

"Well heck-in-a-handbasket, it's true. If you want to chase ghosts and lies, keep looking for a note. If you want to figure out why Mysterio died, you can follow me."

"General Custer had a last stand and he died," I said.

"I'm General Betty."

"Betty Custer?"

"Would you cut it out? You're giving me a headache. This is how I see it. Someone wanted that dragon but Mysterio beat them to it. They then killed Mysterio hoping to get the creature for themselves. But somehow, you and I ended up on the scene, so they either hid or fled. Then you got the dragon and are sent on this stupid wild goose chase about a note. And now someone figures the best way to steal the dragon is if they make it look like the creature's a loose cannon."

I rose. "It's a dragon! It *is* a loose cannon."

Betty and Hugo stared at me. Hugo's mouth drooped, making me feel like a horrible Mama. Which I was because I thought my baby familiar was a demon sent from hell to kill the populace.

I mean, was it that far off?

I inhaled another cleansing breath and rubbed my temples. I dropped to the chair. "Hattie Hollypop's cat confirmed that Donovan bought the dragon for me, making your original theory correct. Now, I'm not saying Mysterio wasn't killed for the dragon—there could be something there. Perhaps someone is trying to get Hugo. What do you propose we do about it?"

Betty smacked the poker onto the map where we had discovered Mysterio. "Here. The scene of the crime. That's where we need to begin our investigation."

"You realize there are cops who do this sort of thing."

"I've told you before—this town would implode if it weren't for me."

That might be true. The week before, when Betty had been in jail under suspicion of murder, she'd had me perform the dirty tasks that kept the town in check. Including guard the Magnolia Cove werewolf to make sure he didn't escape from his chain.

Needless to say, that had gone completely wrong. Not only had I managed to let the werewolf escape, I also uncovered his identity.

Axel Reign.

My kind of boyfriend even though we were cooling our engines. Too bad he was one hot guy who looked amazing in clothes, kissed like a warrior with a gentle streak, and carried jelly beans in his pockets in case I was out.

Yeah. That guy.

Boy, I really need some space from him.

Anyway, Axel was a werewolf, which didn't bother me as much as it bothered him. I know, I know, my life's complicated. I've got a werewolf for a boyfriend, a dragon for a familiar and General Custer for a grandma.

It was lucky I was still sane.

Resigned, I studied Betty, who was learning the board as if she were about to be tested on it. "Okay, so what do you suggest we do?"

She stroked her chin. "We need to get to the heart of the matter and to do that, there's a place we need to inspect. See if there are any clues."

"What place? I've already searched Mysterio's room, where I found the ripped note about my mother, I'd like to add."

"Not there. Someplace else."

"Where?"

Betty rubbed her fingers and smiled. "We need to get into Mysterio's van."

My eyebrows rose. "The van? How're we supposed to do that?"

"We have to steal the key."

I facepalmed my forehead. "And where exactly are we going to steal the key from?"

Betty's mouth spread wide into a devilish grin. "From the police station."

"Are you kidding?"

Betty shook her head. "Nope. And you're the one who's going to nab it."

FOURTEEN

So that's how I found myself standing outside the police station with Betty in tow. "Why aren't we using magic to break into the van?"

"Won't work," Betty said gruffly. "The cops will have warded the vehicle against it. We need the key."

I rubbed my temples, wishing to be a thousand miles away. "What's your plan, exactly?"

She glanced around as if we were up to no good, which did not make me feel confident that we were going to come anywhere close to succeeding. "Wait. We're waiting for someone."

"Who?"

"What's all this about?" My cousin Cordelia strode up wearing a black linen jacket and jeans. She pulled her long hair over one shoulder and eyed the police station with what appeared to be concern.

"Great, you're here," Betty said, clapping her on the arm. "You have to be the distraction so Pepper can grab the key."

"Oh, Lord," I said.

Cordelia rolled her eyes. "What's going on?"

Betty grabbed both of our wrists and yanked us into the bushes. In broad daylight. Nothing suspicious about three grown women hiding in bushes in front of a police station. We probably looked like three hookers trying to figure out how to bust our pimp out of jail.

Scratch that—Betty was with us.

That probably made us look more like hustlers trying to figure out the best way to take down the station.

Yeah, that was it.

She snapped her fingers in my face. "Pay attention."

"I am," I said.

"Your eyes were all glassy like you were thinking about more important things."

"I probably was."

Betty pointed to the building. "I've got it on good authority that Garrick Young has the key to Mysterio's van. It's on his desk, from what I understand, or somewhere around there. Cordelia, you need to pull Garrick away from his office. Then, Pepper, you go in and nab the key. It's easy to spot. It's got black rubber covering the head of it."

"How do you know that?"

"I saw it when Mysterio died," she said. "Should've grabbed it then. Listen, you two go in together, Cordelia—pull Garrick out and Pepper you're in. Got it?"

I blinked at Betty. "And what are you going to do while the two of us are getting ourselves incarcerated?"

"I'll be supervising from here."

"That sounds fair," Cordelia said. "I'll try, but I don't know if I can get him away from his desk."

"You think I don't know about the two of you?" Betty said.

Cordelia flushed red. My jaw dropped.

"Okay," Cordelia said, "we'll be right back."

She grabbed my arm and yanked me from the bushes.

"Garrick?" I said, dumbfounded.

Cordelia slanted her gaze from mine. "Why do you sound so surprised?"

"Oh. I'm not. I guess I'm not. Okay, I am. I didn't see that one coming."

She fisted her hands. "It burns my butt that Betty figured it out. She thinks she's so darn smart. Always one step ahead of everyone. I swear. Trying to keep a secret from her is like trying to keep one from God—impossible."

I smacked my lips. "I wouldn't even try if I were you."

She laughed. It sounded a bit maniacal, like she was on the verge of needing a straightjacket or a bottle of whiskey. Maybe all she needed was some of that honeysuckle wine and she'd be okay. I decided to suggest it once we retrieved the key.

We reached the door. She exhaled. "Garrick will kill me if he finds out we stole the key."

I smiled brightly. "Don't worry. It's not you. It's me. Remember?"

"Same thing practically, except for our hair color."

I laughed. "Come on."

We swept inside and I followed Cordelia to Garrick's office. Wow. She must've already visited him at his office because she led me straight there.

She knocked on the door and Garrick answered. I shrank away as Cordelia pulled him from the office.

"Everything okay?" Garrick said.

Cordelia shook her head. "There's something I need to talk to you about."

I stayed out of sight as Garrick said, "Let's go to the back."

They drifted off. I glanced around the office to make sure no one was looking in my direction. My heart hammered against my chest and blood rushed through my ears. Dear Lord, I would be burned toast if anyone saw me do this.

But no one was looking.

Perfect.

I did a quick search-and-destroy eyeballing of Garrick's desk and spotted the keys. I took a quick step in, snatched them from the desk and shoved them in my pocket.

I turned around and bumped into a rock hard chest.

I sucked in air as a whirlwind of butterflies kicked up in my stomach. Two hands grabbed my shoulders.

"Whoa, there."

I exhaled as Axel righted me. "What're you doing back here?"

He quirked a brow. "Back? Yeah. I left. Returned to talk to the sheriff."

"You mean Garrick?"

His eyes widened. "That's the one."

Was he playing around? He knew Garrick from before the sheriff ever came to Magnolia Cove.

I decided to ignore how weird Axel had been acting lately and scat.

I opened my mouth, but I couldn't tell him I was stealing a key so I could break into Mysterio's impounded vehicle.

What in the world would he think of me?

He'd probably think that I was doing crazy Betty Craple's dirty work, which would be a thousand percent right.

I spoke quickly. "Anyway, I'm not doing anything. Cordelia came in to ask a question and she grabbed Garrick, who said he needed a pen. Oh, here's one." I yanked it from the desk and pivoted around him. "Oh look. I see Cordelia at the door. I don't think she needed one after all."

He rubbed his neck. "See you around."

I gave him a limp wave. "Yeah. See you around."

That was weird. Really weird. Axel acted like he didn't even know me.

I slinked out of the office and nearly left a trail of fire in my wake as I rushed from the station. Once outside, warm air hit my sweating skin. In the time it had taken me to enter the station and nab the key, my crimson hair had plastered to my neck. I'm sure I looked like a late summer hot mess of perspiration.

I found Betty down the street. "Did you get it?"

"Yes."

She opened her palm. "Hand it over."

"No way. I'm keeping it. You can't send me in to do your dirty work and expect to get the prize."

"I'm old."

I glared at her. "I don't care. I almost got caught by Axel."

She frowned. "What's he doing in there?"

I paused. "I didn't ask."

Betty's brows pinched together as her eyes narrowed. "Never mind. Let's hope he doesn't blow the whistle and tell Garrick that he found you in the office. Even if he does, we'll do the one thing we can."

"What's that?"

"Deny it."

Sounded about as perfect as the rest of this plan. But I had to hand it to Betty, the scheme worked. So far. Definitely something I needed to keep reminding myself.

Cordelia huffed as she strode up to us. "I hope you got the key. I had to make up some crazy story."

"About what?" I said.

My cousin threaded her fingers through the ends of her hair nervously. She puckered her mouth into a little bow before grimacing. "I had to tell him—I forget what I told him."

With the air of authority that you get from being old and ornery, Betty said, "You told him you were feeling the pressure about your relationship. That you needed to make a decision between him and Zach because it was beginning to be too much and your feelings were becoming too tangled and deep."

Cordelia glared at her. "What I said is none of your business."

Betty poked the air. "But I'm right. I always am."

Cordelia grabbed her arm. "Come on. Let's get out of here before anyone puts two and two together."

We made our way to Betty's house, where we took up shop on the screened-in back porch. Betty magicked up a pitcher of sweet tea and several glasses. When we were settled on the wicker furniture with sugary goodness flowing through our veins, Betty started.

"I haven't told Amelia about this plan."

"What plan?" Amelia said, popping her head into the room.

"The one where Betty gets us all incarcerated," I said.

"Ooh, sounds like fun," she said, pulling up a chair and helping herself to some tea.

"It's where we discover who killed Mysterio and who wants Pepper's dragon."

I rolled my eyes. "I'm not convinced anyone wants my dragon. You're the one who thinks that."

"I agree with Pepper," Cordelia said.

"You'll both see," Betty said. "Amelia, you can be the lookout tonight."

"Great. I didn't have any plans anyway."

Betty settled her gaze on Cordelia and me. "The two of you will search the van while I do the instructing."

"What exactly are we looking for?" Cordelia said.

"I don't know," Betty admitted.

I shook my head in annoyance. "This is worse than trying to find a needle in the haystack. And where's the car impounded? Please don't tell me behind the police station."

Betty's eyes shifted left and right. "You'll have to be quiet."

Cordelia scoffed. "Why am I doing this again?"

"To keep your cousin from being murdered."

I shot up. "Murdered? How did this suddenly become I'm going to be murdered? Have you lost your Cracker Jacks? Or did you even have any to begin with?"

Betty squared her shoulders. "I didn't want to say it, but I think it's got to come on out. Mysterio may have been murdered for that dragon. You, Pepper, now own the dragon. If my theory is correct, then whoever killed Mysterio will likely come after you. See, I'm connecting A to B to C."

"I think you're connecting Venus and Mars instead of letters," I said. "That makes absolutely no sense. Donovan bought the dragon for me."

Betty crossed her arms. "He did buy it for you, but perhaps someone knew about it and resolved to kill for it."

"I agree with Pepper," Cordelia said. "There's no evidence for any of this craziness."

"That's why we're infiltrating the van," Amelia said pertly.

Cordelia and I shot her hard glances. Amelia shrugged. "What?

Crazier things have happened. She might be right. We check the van for clues, if we don't find any we lock Betty up in a first witch's home."

Betty clapped her hands and Amelia's tea disappeared. Amelia rose. "Someone come get me when it's time. I'll be waiting and ready."

I spent the rest of the afternoon running to Familiar Place and feeding and watering the animals. When I wasn't around, they went into a state of suspended animation, which made caring for them easier. But I hated leaving them like that for long. I wanted to take Hugo out, but after the earlier run-in, I wasn't sure what to do. He needed more training, and to be honest, I still wasn't sure I was the right witch for him. I did feel a connection, but I couldn't have him scorching animals or people.

Clearly, that would be a problem.

I locked up my shop and headed to the house. The sun burned down the horizon. Betty would be rearing to go pretty soon.

I found her sitting by the hearth, stirring some black liquid in a cauldron. "Is Barry the Dragon Tamer still around?"

Betty tapped the spoon against the iron. "I believe so. Need more training?"

"I need about as much training as I can get. Or at least a manual. I have no idea how I'm supposed to raise a dragon. It's not like there are YouTube videos on it."

Betty drummed her fingers on the chair. "I'll talk to Barry, see if he can get you more time. That's if you manage to stay alive long enough to keep hold of the dragon."

I gritted my teeth. "Will you knock off the whole 'someone wants to murder you' thing? It's getting old."

Not to mention every time she mentioned it my gut clenched and I felt the urge to use the bathroom.

"It's the truth. I'm trying to keep you on your toes. Make sure you're battle-ready."

"Oh, I'm battle-ready."

"If you mean a battle against ants, you might be right. But against people? Someone like Rufus? You'd be toast, kid."

I rolled my eyes.

Cordelia and Amelia strolled into the room. "It's starting to get late. The station's quiet on Sundays," Cordelia said.

"Oh? Know firsthand?" Betty said.

Cordelia ignored her.

Amelia glanced in the pot. "What are you cooking?"

Betty scooped out a ladle of inky liquid. "This is your makeup for tonight. It'll keep folks from seeing you."

"It looks like tar," I said. "Smells like it to. You sure that's safe?"

Betty smiled. "You're about to find out. It's go time."

FIFTEEN

*T*he four of us sneaked into the lot behind the police station. We had all piled into my old Camry, which I'd barely driven since I'd been in town as I didn't have any use for it.

The moon had shifted into its crescent form, spilling light onto several parked cars. I stared at the street lamps.

"Those might be a problem. Mysterio's van is parked directly beneath one."

"Which is his?" Amelia asked.

I pointed to the van with the black hat teetering atop it. "That's the one."

"Oh," Amelia said in a way that made me think she'd realized that if it had been a snake, the van would've bitten her.

"The lights won't be any problem." Betty clapped her hands. The lamps winked out.

"How long will that last?" Cordelia said.

"About twenty minutes. Plenty of time to find what we're looking for."

"Even though we don't know what that is," I said.

"Right. But when you find it, you'll know it. I trust your instincts."

I glanced in the mirror. Smudges of black lined my cheeks and forehead. "I'm not sure what I trust at this point cause I'm betting this stuff is going to leave a mark so dark I won't be able to leave the house for days."

Betty waved dismissively. "All it needs is soap and water."

"So she says," Cordelia said, shoving open the door. "Come on. Time's wasting. Amelia, you're on guard, right?"

Amelia saluted us. "Aye, aye, captain. I'm your watch."

"Let's go," Cordelia said.

We slinked from the car, leaving Betty in the driver's seat. It occurred to me that if we were caught, Betty could just drive away, leaving us stranded.

"You don't think she'll desert us if the going gets tough, do you?" I said to Cordelia.

"Anything's possible."

"That doesn't make me feel better."

Amelia wrapped an arm around my shoulder. "Betty loves us. She wouldn't leave us high and dry." She paused. "I don't think."

"We'd better hurry," I said.

Amelia took a stance where she could see the rear of the police station as well as if anyone pulled into the lot. I slid the key into the door.

"Alarm?" I said.

Cordelia flattened her palms on the side. "I'm on it."

I turned the key until I heard the lock *snick*. I pulled the doors open.

"Holy geez," Cordelia said.

"You can say that again."

We gave each other oh-crap looks. "Fifteen minutes. I want to be out way before those lights come on. Let's go."

"Where?" she said. "Where do we even start?"

"I'll take the front. You take the back."

Mysterio's van looked like a studio apartment crammed with everything ever created by mankind.

I'm not kidding.

There were statues and papers, bookshelves and dressers, a filing cabinet and a large chest. There was simply so much that fifteen minutes wouldn't even put a dent in the amount of sheer *stuff* we'd have to shuffle through.

I wiggled my way to the front, where Mysterio's bed was bolted down. Costumes and clothes lined the head and foot, hanging from a rod suspended from the ceiling. I lifted the mattress but found nothing. I riffled through clothes and started on a desk beside the bed.

The drawers were unlocked. I opened the first one and discovered a manila folder stuffed with purchase orders.

And then I found it. Like, literally five seconds in I found a receipt for a dragon. But it wasn't from my shop. It was some shop in Florida. It looked like Mysterio had purchased the dragon about a month or so earlier.

"Look at this," I said.

Cordelia crawled over. "What?"

"It looks like Mysterio purchased a dragon from a store in Florabama."

"Florabama? The beach?"

"Yeah. But if he purchased a dragon from them, why would he have needed to purchase my dragon?"

"Maybe he's not very good with them. Some don't last long in captivity, right?"

I tapped the page. "That's true, but I don't know. It's weird. Let's see what else there is."

I kept digging and sure enough, I found more receipts from several different shops located all across the country. All for the purchase of dragons.

"Who is this guy? Does he have some dragon fetish?"

"I don't know. The whole thing's weird. And of course, there's nothing here about my mother."

Cordelia gave me a sad smile. "I didn't think there would be. Do you think that was Aunt Sassafras up there on stage? It looked like her, but I just don't believe Mysterio. Sorry. I had to say it."

My hopes plummeted to my feet. "I don't know." I sighed so hard my shoulders slumped. "Maybe I want the whole thing to be more than what it really is."

"Pssst, y'all. Someone's coming."

Amelia's voice snapped me back to the present. I stuffed several of the invoices into my shirt because I had no place else to put them. I hopped out of the van right behind Cordelia and shut the doors quietly.

Amelia came around the corner. "Whew. That was close. I saw that Garrick guy glance outside at the lights that are out. Then he ducked in. I didn't know if he'd come out, but I figured we'd better be safe than sorry."

We crept to the car and slid inside. I glanced around but there was no sign of Garrick.

"What'd you find?" Betty said.

"It's a conspiracy," I said. "Mysterio killed JFK and then hired a crapload of dragons to run the stock market. That actually goes pretty well most of the time, but sometimes it crashes."

"You're a bad granddaughter," she said.

I laughed. "Come on. Let's get home and we'll tell you all about it."

Once we were inside, Betty dropped her purse on the empty chair. "Okay, what'd you find out?"

I pulled the papers out from under my shirt and smacked them on the coffee table. "Apparently Mysterio was going around buying up dragons."

Betty picked up the papers. "Well, well, well. My girls, the super sleuths," she said proudly.

"Thank you," I said brightly. "So what was he doing with the dragons?"

"Selling them," Betty said. "Buying low and selling high—probably to folks on the black market."

"Whoa. You just jumped from A to Z again."

Amelia thumbed dirt out from under her fingernails. "She might not be wrong. I've read that selling magical creatures can be big business. But how do we discover his contacts? And why would someone kill Mysterio?"

Betty scratched her chin. "Those are the answers we need if we're going to save Pepper's life."

"Not this again." I raked my fingers under my eyes, getting globs of black gunk under the nails. I sighed. "I seriously doubt anyone's going to kill me because I own the dragon. And I also don't think the scorching in the park was planned and that I'm marked for death."

"That would be a great movie title," Amelia said. "*Marked for Death*."

"It *is* a movie," Cordelia said.

Amelia rolled her eyes. "But what if our grandmother's right? If Mysterio was murdered because of the dragon, then the killer may come after you, Pepper. There's no way to be sure until we catch whoever that is. And right now we're short on leads."

We stared at each other. Tension filled the room like fog. Betty pointed toward the sky. "I always think better when I'm cooking. Who wants some cobbler?"

"Me," Amelia said.

"I'll pass," Cordelia said.

"I'm on the edge," I said. "I think I've gained weight since I arrived."

"You can't tell," Amelia said.

"Thanks."

Betty smacked her lips. "I'll cook. That'll help."

Fire crackled in the hearth. Betty whipped up a skillet filled with blackberries and topped it with batter.

"I'm going to wash my face," I said.

I excused myself to the bathroom, where I scrubbed off the thick black sludge. I had been right. Dark streaks marred my skin. I shook my head and hoped Betty would get them off before work tomorrow morning.

When I jogged downstairs, I found Betty with one shoulder pressed against the wall. She pulled the corncob pipe from her pocket and lit it. Thick smoke drifted to the ceiling.

"Is that your thinking stance?" I said.

She nodded. "It helps."

"Okay, so if we figure Mysterio was selling, who was he selling to?"

Betty frowned. "That's what we have to discover."

"A dragon would certainly stand out," I said. "Unless they weren't selling the dragons. Some cultures sell dragon bones for medicinal purposes. Do you think that's the case?"

Amelia chirped from her spot on the couch. "That's a good possibility."

"Hmm." I nibbled the inside of my lip. When I glanced up, I caught Cordelia studying me. "What is it? Oh, I know this hideous black stuff is stuck on my face."

She shook his head. "No. I was just wondering if it would come off my face, too."

"Here's to hoping," I croaked, sounding more like a frog about to be frog-gigged in the middle of the night than a woman with black crap slashed across her skin.

We stared at each other in silence until it hit me.

I snapped my fingers. "There's one man in town who knows about dragons, and who has quite a few of them himself. He may know the answers."

Betty's eyes flared. "Barry."

I smiled. "Right. Have you set up a meeting for tomorrow?"

She smiled. "I'll do it right now."

I grinned. "All right. We need to put a list of questions together for me to grill him on. Let's get moving. It's already getting late."

SIXTEEN

*I*t only took a few minutes for Betty to get ahold of Barry and set up a meeting for the next morning. She worked her magic in about five minutes.

Luckily that magic didn't include her snorting sparkles from her nose.

Anyway, we came up with a strategy for approaching Barry and then all of us headed off to bed. I went upstairs, rubbed Mattie's head and gave Hugo a good stroke before snuggling under the comforter and setting off into dreamland.

I awoke the next morning ready to tackle my class with Barry. We had set up the meeting for eight am. I showered, dressed and grabbed a light bite to eat before pulling Hugo from the cage and heading off to the same park where Barry and I had worked before.

When I saw him, he was dressed in his lederhosen and doing squats.

"Good morning," I said.

"Morning," Barry said. "How're things going with Hugo?"

I smiled. "You remember his name."

"I always remember a dragon's name. It's important." Barry gave the dragon a good scratch on the head. Hugo's tongue lolled and his eyes closed in pleasure.

"Why is it so important?"

Barry's brown eyes flecked with interest. "Dragons are highly intelligent. They know when you like them and when you don't. Bonding with them, even if the creature isn't your familiar is still important—you have to earn a dragon's respect."

He gave Hugo one last pat and glanced at me. "So. How's it been going?"

"Not great," I admitted. "Yesterday he dive-bombed some cats and dogs who were fighting. Sent out a spray of fire, too."

Barry grimaced. "Oh my goodness. That is truly terrible. Truly a horrible thing. Tell me, what could have set off this majestic creature to want to destroy a little puffball of a cat?"

"I don't know. I was hoping maybe you'd have some answers, because I certainly don't."

"I was not there, so I can't contribute any help for that particular situation." He paused. "Did Hugo believe you to be in any trouble?"

"I don't think so. I believe he wanted to stop the fight, but it caused a bigger problem. Now this baby is being seen as a menace to society. I was warned to keep him on a tight leash or else."

"Or else what?"

"The cops will have to take him from me."

"Tsk, tsk, tsk. The majesty of such a creature cannot be contained. It is impossible to even suggest such a thing."

I licked my lips and stepped forward. "But you, Barry. You have dragons and you keep them safe and from hurting people. At least, I assume so."

"Yes, yes. I have many dragons though I've worked with them for years to make them as tame as possible. But dragons are very smart. They do not attack without a reason."

"How have you done that?"

Barry crossed his arms and splayed his legs. "The dragon must want to protect you, but also understand what is a real threat and what isn't. That's part of the bond. You simply don't have the concrete bond yet."

"But isn't there any other training?" I bit on my fingers, trying to look worried and scared. "I'm afraid that if something else happens and Hugo freaks out, the witches will want his head. Literally."

Barry grimaced. "Such an awful image." He shrugged. "All we can do is strengthen the bond. Tighten it to the point where the two of you are one mind."

I shifted my weight. "That's all we can do? You don't think Hugo might be better served in a different community? A different place?"

Barry shook his head. "Perhaps that will happen in time. But you must give it all you've got first. Control the beast, don't let the beast control you." He inhaled a deep shot of air. "Now. Are you ready?"

"Sure. I'm ready."

"Now, throw Hugo up in the air and catch him."

"Say what?"

"It will create the bond."

So I threw my dragon in the air until my arms shook with fatigue. This little guy already weighed a good ten pounds. I would toss him high and then Hugo fluttered his wings, sailing down until he landed softly in my arms. I'd heave him up again and he'd float back.

By the tenth time or so, I started to feel the string again, the connection between us.

Barry must've noticed it too. "Now tell him to fly into the trees and back. Tell him with your thoughts."

I frowned. I always spoke to animals with my mouth, not my head. But I did it.

To the trees.

Hugo took off like an arrow. "Holy cow," I said. The dragon shot off. Branches splintered and cracked as he dove in.

"Tell him to return," Barry said. Then he threw me a dead mouse.

"Yuck."

"You must reward him."

To me, I thought.

Branches twisted and snapped as Hugo returned. He dove toward me. Freaked out, I threw the mouse into the air. Hugo snatched it in his beak and swallowed it whole. The dragon then came to rest on my arm.

I stared at the creature and glanced at Barry, who smiled widely. "That is the first step. You're creating the bond and once the bond is sealed, it won't be broken and your dragon will be tame to the point where he won't even breathe unless you say it's okay."

"That seems a little extreme."

Barry laughed. "Meet me tomorrow morning and we'll keep working."

We started to leave. "Barry."

He quirked a brow. "Yes?"

"What if Hugo staying here in Magnolia Cove puts him in more danger than it's worth?"

Barry's expression darkened. "Then we will discuss it when that happens. But not now. I know people who will take him and they will pay plenty. But only if it's your last option."

"Thanks. That's all I needed to know."

We went our separate ways, and I wondered exactly what Barry could do in a few days to help me raise a dragon. Because I wasn't sure what could be done to keep this little guy under my thumb.

Was that even possible? I mean we're talking about a dragon.

But anyway, we left the park and I took Hugo with me to Familiar Place. I snapped on the light. The cats yawned, the puppies yipped and the birds chirped as they woke. I put Hugo on the floor, where he sniffed as he explored the territory.

Betty entered as soon as the clock struck ten. "Well? What'd you find out?"

I took a foam cup of coffee that she extended from her hand. "Not much. I tried prodding Barry to see if he knew anyone who would take Hugo if I had to give him up, but he wasn't that helpful. He didn't offer any names."

Betty frowned. "Think he's hiding something?"

I shrugged. "Hard to say. I don't know. But he certainly didn't jump on the bandwagon of taking the dragon, either. If he's aware of some sort of black market for selling them, he's not talking."

"I bet I could've found out."

I folded my arms and leaned one hip against the counter. "So you're saying that if we had sent you in instead of me, you could've discovered the real truth that Barry the Dragon Tamer is hiding?"

"Of course. I run this town, don't I?"

"Doesn't mean you run the world."

"You'd be surprised." Betty sipped her coffee. "So we're back to square one."

"Not really. Mysterio had contacts in Magnolia Cove. Someone might know something; I just don't know what."

Betty raised her cup. "Let me know if that boyfriend of yours comes up with a plan. We've got to keep you safe."

I discreetly avoided acknowledging the boyfriend comment.

"I am safe. Rufus isn't getting into town anytime soon."

Betty scowled. "You know what I mean. I'm not talking about Rufus. I'm talking about whoever here in town wants to harm you to get to that dragon."

I dismissed her with a wave. "I'll be extra careful. How's that sound?"

"Good." Betty tossed her cup in the trash bin. She pulled her pipe from her pocket and stared out the window. "There's that Hattie Hollypop."

My eyebrows shot up. "Hattie! I totally forgot."

"Forgot what?"

I smirked. "With all your craziness about someone wanting to steal Hugo and whatnot, I forgot Hattie told me she could help me discover the message Mom had for me."

"And you believe her?"

"I believe her about as much as I believe someone wants to kill me."

"Hmpf."

I strode toward the door. "Can you watch the store for me? Only for a few minutes. I want to talk to Hattie."

Betty pulled her corncob pipe from her mouth and lit it from a flame that appeared on the tip of her finger. Wow. If that didn't appear so scary, I would actually say that it was cool. "Go on. I'll be here."

I nearly catapulted from the store to catch up with Hattie. Turned out, I didn't. I walked all the way to Brews and Jewels, and ended up following her inside.

I had no idea why I'd never entered this store before. The first thing I saw was a handcrafted silver and amethyst necklace that took every breath I had from my body. And I mean every breath—past and present. The piece was stunning.

In fact, the whole store was filled with cases of richly colored gemstones set in either silver or gold.

"Wow," I said.

Hattie, who'd taken a spot behind the counter, smiled at me. She'd tamed her hair into a coiffed gorgeous up-do. Her dark eyeshadow matched the jewel tones of the gems sprinkled around the shop. I peeked beyond her and noticed the bar.

There were already a few people drinking wine.

Hey, who was I to judge?

"So you decided to come," Hattie said.

I dragged my gaze from an emerald ring to her. "This store is amazing. I can't believe I've never been in before. Of course, my pocketbook wouldn't like it very much," I said, laughing in embarrassment. "But boy, I could spend a fortune here."

"Lots of people could and do," she said, still smiling.

I strode up to the counter, keeping my hands plastered to my sides so that I didn't touch anything. Last thing I needed to do was break a valuable that cost my entire year's income. Boy, I'd be in deep trouble then. I was pretty sure this place had a You-Break-It-You-Buy-It policy.

"Is your dragon okay?" she asked.

"He's fine, though that little fire-breathing stint caused me some problems with the law. He's young and I'm still learning how to bond with him and whatnot." I rolled my eyes. "To be honest, I'm not sure if

I'm cut out to own a dragon. There's a lot of responsibility that goes with that."

Hattie smiled. "That's one thing I don't have to worry about with a cat."

"Too bad I couldn't bond with one of those," I said.

She laughed and held my gaze for a long moment. "So. What can I help you with?"

"Yes. Do you remember when I mentioned I was trying to figure out about that message my mother had left with Mysterio?"

"Of course. Are you here to see if we can figure it out?"

I pulled the folded sheet from my purse. Yes, I had it with me. There was no way I was going to separate myself from it. After all, it was the closest thing I had to a message from my dead mother. I didn't want it far from me at all.

Hattie pressed the page onto the counter. She pursed her lips as she rubbed the writing. "There are some things I can try. I'm not sure if they'll work, but it may help shed some light anyway."

Hope bubbled in my chest. "Oh? What things?"

Hattie slid open a case and pulled out a rough looking ebony stone. She slid it over the page. Then she looked up and smiled. "Sometimes the burned bat's bone does the trick. Sometimes it doesn't. Let's see."

I leaned back, horrified. "Burned bat's bones?"

"Yes. Some of the precious stones in this shop aren't stones at all. They're actually bones or other organic substances."

"Other organic substances?" I said, no less grossed out by what she was implying.

"Things like petrified dove hearts, dried lizard livers, that sort of thing. They're all hard as stone, even if they aren't technically rock. The uses for such things is myriad."

The edges of the paper began to smoke. Worry knotted my stomach. "What's happening? That thing isn't going to destroy the page, is it?"

"It shouldn't." Hattie waved her hand over the paper until the smoke cleared. The page looked exactly as it had before.

"What are you trying to do?"

Hattie tapped her fingers on the glass as she searched the contents of the case. "I'm trying to return what was written on that page to it. I guess the bat's bones didn't work. We might have to pull out the big guns."

My eyebrows rose. "The big guns?"

"I'm thinking an owl's eye."

"Ew."

She laughed. "It's only called that."

"Thank goodness."

"It's really an owl's testicle."

I nearly vomited. "Gross."

Hattie rubbed a white marble over the page. This time the paper curled and flexed as if warming up for a sprint.

"I think I might throw up before I leave this place."

Hattie laughed. "You wouldn't be the first person that's happened to."

The paper stopped twisting. I leaned over to see if any writing had appeared. "Nothing again."

Hattie poked the air. "Don't worry. I'm not giving up. The third's the charm, right?"

"So they say."

She pulled a blood red stone from another case. She rubbed it between her palms before setting it on the page.

I shoved the phone in my pocket as a spark burst from the page. I ducked to the floor, covering my head. "Holy crap! What was that?"

Hattie leaned over the counter, where I cowered like a big pansy. "That was the bloodstone at work. Come see what was written."

I pressed a hand to my heart, where my chest hammered against my palm. I took several deep gulps of air and pushed up to standing.

The paper sparkled and glistened. I stared at the words. My body filled with joy as I gazed on more of the text. Letters hovered in the space where they would normally have been if the rest of page had existed. But instead of paper, it was ink floating in the atmosphere—ink and handwriting that perfectly matched the beginning of the text.

Tell her that though we are separated, there is something she must know. The depth—

My chest deflated. "What? Is that it? Where's the rest of the message?"

Hattie shot me a sympathetic frown. "I'm sorry. That's all that written. The bloodstone revealed everything that was on the page before it had been ripped off. Was there something else you wanted or expected?"

I stared at the paper and realized that Mysterio must've been interrupted when he wrote the message.

I sighed. All my hope and joy vanished in less than an instant. "I didn't know what to expect. I had hoped the message would've been complete, but it's not."

I glanced at the stone and a new thread of thought flared. "Are you sure that stone is right? That there isn't more? I mean, maybe that stone is defunct or something."

Hattie laughed as if I'd said the most asinine thing since someone suggested that slicing bread was a horrible idea.

Not sure if that ever happened, but it sounded reasonable.

"There's no way the bloodstone is wrong. It's the most accurate artifact I have."

I cocked a brow. "What makes you so sure?"

Hattie's lips coiled into a smug smile. "Because of what it's created from. Blood from the purest and most magical creature that has ever been known to exist."

I shoved a hand on my hip. "Just because it's so magical doesn't mean it's right. Maybe it missed something. Can you try again?"

"I'm sorry to disappoint you. I know this was important, but the bloodstone is never wrong. It just never is. I wish I could say that there's been a time that doing the spell twice worked, but it didn't. The bloodstone did its job."

I sighed. "Okay. I guess that's it, then." I flashed her a feeble smile, knowing I'd come to the end of the road about the message my mother had left me. "Thanks."

I shouldered my purse and headed toward the door. I paused

before opening it and turned to Hattie. "And just what was that blood-stone made of?"

Hattie polished the rock before placing it carefully in the case. "That particular bloodstone is made of the heart of a magical creature."

"Right. You said magical creature, but which one?"

My blood froze when Hattie said, "Why, a dragon, of course."

SEVENTEEN

I trembled the entire walk to Familiar Place. When I got inside, there was a young woman with shoulder-length brown hair browsing the merchandise.

"I've got a nice iguana in the back," Betty offered.

"I'm looking for a Maine coon cat."

"How about a nice basset hound? I'm sure we can order one of those for you," Betty said.

I nearly smacked my forehead. I strolled up to the woman and smiled. "I'd be happy to order a Maine coon for you, but we can't guarantee a match with a familiar sight unseen. I'm afraid you'll be disappointed. You never know what sort of familiar you're going to connect with."

My gaze shifted to Hugo, who slept on a towel that Betty had obviously tossed in a corner for him.

The woman sniffed. "I have my heart set on a Maine coon."

"Those are stupid cats," one of the kittens said. "Send her my way."

I peered over the woman's shoulder at a long-haired silver tabby. "Why don't you look at this little guy?"

The woman's nose wrinkled. I led her over to the cage and said, "What do you think?"

"I don't know," she said.

Then lightning struck. Not literally, but kinda sorta. The woman's gaze met the cat's and the rest was history.

Ten minutes later, another satisfied customer exited Familiar Place. Betty brushed her hands. "Another successful pairing thanks to me."

I nearly choked on her lie. "Are you kidding? If it had been up to you, she would've ended up with a bumblebee for a familiar."

"Is that a problem?"

"Yes. Especially since we don't sell them."

"A minor inconvenience."

I flared my arms. "Okay. Whatever, but I think I may have discovered something pretty serious."

"What's that?"

"Hattie Hollypop has a store filled with stones that are taken from the body parts of animals."

"That's what some witches use for spell casting. Why?"

I grabbed a bottle of water from behind the counter and drank half of it. "Because one of the stones she had was made from a dragon."

Betty's eyebrows shot to peaks. "My, my. Now that is interesting."

"Yeah, but I don't know what to do with it."

"Did you ask her where it came from?"

Oh, crap. "No, I didn't. I wasn't thinking straight. She said dragon; my body went all wonky on me. It was very strange. But I feel like that's a solid lead. Remember, I saw her with Mysterio. She knew him. He could've been buying dragons for some horrible trade that makes magical stones from them. Then Hattie was buying the stones." I clapped my hands together as if I'd solved the case. "See? It's perfect."

The bell tinkled. "What's perfect?"

Cordelia entered carrying two boxed plates of food. "We had some left over lunch from a party. Thought I'd drop it by."

"You're my favorite granddaughter today," Betty said.

I smirked.

Cordelia shook her head. "I'm not looking for brownie points."

Betty opened it and dug into the plate filled with chicken, pimiento and fruit salad. I smiled as Cordelia handed me a box.

"Thank you."

"So what no-good thing are y'all up to?" Cordelia said.

I plucked a cranberry from the chicken salad and popped it in my mouth. "Hattie Hollypop has a dragon bloodstone."

Cordelia whistled. "Wow. Now that's something I didn't expect. A dragon bloodstone? You think she's in on the whole dragon selling ring?"

Betty raised a fork full of salad. "Why don't we tie Hugo outside her jewelry shop and see if she steals him? We'll hide out and yell 'gotcha' when Hattie nabs him."

I swiveled in a chair toward her. "That's a teensy bit too crazy even for me."

"You're the sane one."

"Oh, that's right."

Cordelia inspected a long strand of her blond hair. "Grandma Betty's got a good point. If this whole thing is about dragon buying, then there are several ways we can go."

Betty poked the air with her fork. "Cordelia's right. We can one, bait the killer. Two, don't bait the killer and wait for them to come to you. Or three, we bait the killer."

My stomach coiled. "I take it you think we should bait the killer."

A slow smile spread across Betty's face. "That's a great idea, and I've got the perfect plan to make sure it happens."

Cordelia studied her. "You're not thinking what I think you're thinking, are you?"

"If you're thinking we should stage something that showcases Hugo but also makes him vulnerable, then you're exactly right."

I frowned. "But what? What are we supposed to stage?"

Cordelia groaned. "Our grandmother wants us to stage a helpless creature nearly being eaten by a baby dragon."

I shook my head. "No one's going to buy him eating a creature. We need flames. Flames and fire."

Betty snapped her fingers. "I've got it."

"What's that?"

Her tooth glinted in the sunlight as she smiled. "We set the neighborhood on fire."

"And kill someone?" I screeched. "No way."

She shrugged. "Okay. We'll set our own house on fire then."

I nodded. "That's better."

EIGHTEEN

That afternoon, the three of us worked through the entire set up. We ironed out the wrinkles and even though Betty tried to create more dents in the plan than she smoothed out, we still managed to wrangle her in until we had a sold working outline.

"Okay, one last time," I said.

Betty moved little tuffs of napkin around on the counter as if they were chess pieces. "I'll set a fire here, on the front side of the house. You and your cousins run out screaming that the dragon set the house ablaze. Throw your hands up in the air and look scared." She shot me a pointed look. "Should be easy for you."

I rolled my eyes. "Then what?"

"Then we make a big enough fuss that the neighbors say that the dragon needs to be taken away. We put up a big fight with Garrick about this—"

"—And make an enemy in the meantime," I said.

Cordelia grabbed one of the papers and moved it to the side. "Garrick's not like that."

I rubbed my arms. "Okay, so we don't make an enemy. After Garrick gets called, what do we do?"

Betty plucked the paper from Cordelia's grasp and returned it to its spot. "Then we put up a big fuss that no one's going to take the dragon."

"Okay."

"Then here's the brilliant part," Betty said smugly. "Then we wait. We put the dragon outside as if we're mad at him, as if we're punishing him and we wait."

"Because all that ruckus will ensure we got someone's attention?" I said.

Betty nodded. "The right person's attention."

"Or the wrong one," Cordelia said.

"All that fuss will buzz around the neighborhood faster than a mosquito drinking up the town's blood."

"Gross," I said.

"But it gets to the point," Betty said, shuffling in her chair. "They'll be watching and waiting, thinking their time is near. So that's what we do."

"Okay. When's the plan set for?"

Betty's eyes sparkled. "Tonight."

I ARRIVED home with the dragon draped around my neck. I was beginning to get attached to little Hugo and the more I thought about it, the more I realized that I didn't want any harm to come to this little guy. He was supposed to grow up to be my protector. Well, in the meantime, I was his protector, right? It was my job to make sure he stayed safe.

And I planned on doing that to the utmost.

When I entered the house, I saw that Betty had Cordelia and Amelia on the couch, going over our plans.

Amelia shot me a worried look while I hid a smile.

She raised her hand. "Oh, oh, I want to be the one who screams. I've got a great screaming voice. I know I can make it sound totally real."

"You got it. You're our screamer."

Cordelia yawned. "And even though I helped hatch this plan, I want to be the one who looks bored while the rest of y'all are running around looking like chickens with your heads cut off."

"Not an option," Betty said. "You've got to play or you don't get to witness the festivities."

"Rats. That's what I was afraid of."

I uncoiled Hugo from my neck and rested him on the floor. "So. It looks like y'all are about ready. What time is this thing going down?"

"At twenty-one hundred hours," Betty said.

"What?" Amelia said.

"Nine o'clock," Betty said. "On the nose. I've got my magic ready to go. I need y'all ready to run. We want it to look good, but not fake."

"Should I have curlers in my hair?" Cordelia said. "Maybe wear my fuzzy slippers?"

"Yes to the curlers, no to the fuzzy slippers. I need that grass to feel pokey under your feet."

"I'm going for the slippers," Cordelia said.

"I'm going to wear a giant onesie," Amelia said. "It'll be more dramatic that way."

"I'm wearing jeans and t-shirt," I said. "And no one gets to argue with me about it."

"I'll put on a housecoat," Betty said. "That way at least one of us looks believable."

Cordelia rose and stretched. "Great. Until then, I'm going to work out. I'll be by later for dinner and shenanigans."

"I'll go with you," Amelia said.

They left and Betty pulled the elastic waistband of her pants up under her boobs. "All right. You and me, kid, let's get cracking."

"What are we going to do?"

"Bond you more with your dragon," she said.

"I thought I was working with Barry on that."

She sniffed. "You are, but I want a deeper bond."

I wrapped a hand around Hugo. "He's just a baby. He has to grow and mature. The bond will come."

Betty cracked her knuckles. "Don't worry. I'm not going to play

Dr. Frankenstein on him. All I want to do is make sure he knows you're his mother."

"Why?"

"If someone does nab him, then Hugo will fight to find you. He'll want to get back to you."

"So basically he'll char anyone who steals him?"

"Exactly." Betty clapped her hands and pointed at me. "That's the way we make sure he stays safe."

I frowned. "That sounds like a great idea and all, but I don't want to do that to him. He's only just hatched. This little guy needs to develop naturally. Let's just leave Hugo the way he is."

"Fine," Betty grumbled. "But I don't want you to complain to me when your dragon runs off and forgets all about you."

"I won't." I gave her a Scout's salute "Promise."

The rest of the afternoon into evening flowed smoothly. I worked with Hugo, trying to get him to come to my call and playing fetch with him.

It turned out baby dragons loved fetch.

As the sky darkened and the stars winked overhead, my stomach started churning. We'd made concrete plans for the trap, but I wasn't feeling good about it. In fact, my intestines were coiling from nerves.

Everything would be fine. Betty knew what she was doing. After all, she basically ran this town.

Into its grave.

Nope. Wait. I took deep breaths and shook out my hands. I brought Hugo in from the backyard and found Cordelia in rollers, Amelia in a giant onesie and Betty wearing a housecoat—all as promised.

I glanced at Cordelia. "You know Garrick's probably going to be here, right?"

Her eyes widened. She snapped her fingers and the rollers disappeared. "Good point."

Betty's gaze narrowed on Cordelia but she didn't say anything. "All right. Is everyone ready?"

"No, I'm not," I said. "Where am I supposed to put Hugo during all of this? If he's the one who set the fire, doesn't he need to be around?"

Betty tapped a hand to her mouth. "We'll put him on the porch and then when the fire starts, we'll run him to the back."

Cordelia threaded her fingers through her hair. "Why don't we set the fire in back instead? I mean, what if the blaze gets out of control and hurts Jennie?"

"I wouldn't want anything to happen to Jennie, either," Amelia said. "She's like family, even if she is a guard-vine."

"The back isn't as convenient," Betty said. "It's not front and center for everyone to see."

"How about you set it so that it blazes straight up like an emergency flare?" I suggested.

Betty clapped her hands. "Great idea. It's no wonder you girls are related to me. You're brilliant."

"Or insane," Cordelia said.

"I know I'm at least a little sane," Amelia said.

Cordelia frowned. "That remains to be seen."

Amelia punched her in the arm.

"Ouch."

"Okay, let's get this going," I said. "I'm a bundle of nerves here."

Betty glanced at me. "Place the dragon in the backyard and let me know if anyone's out there."

I did as she said. Stars sprinkled the sky and lights burned on the back porches of the neighbors butting up behind us.

I set Hugo on the lawn. "Stay here. I'll be right back."

"Okay," he said.

I paused. "Okay?"

"Okay, Mama."

"Wow. You've learned to talk fast."

I gave him a pat and returned to my family. "He's in the back and it's all clear."

Betty pulled her pipe from the pocket of her housecoat, slid it between her teeth and lit the bowl with the end of her fingertip. She smiled widely.

"It's go time."

NINETEEN

*B*etty covered one nostril with her finger. A line of sparks from the corncob pipe shot straight up through the ceiling.

"That better not burn anything in my room," Cordelia said.

"Your room's going to be fine," Betty replied. "In three...two...one."

A loud *crack* shook the house. I wobbled to the side as what felt like an earthquake fissured through the living room.

"What was that?" Amelia said.

"Everyone outside," Betty yelled.

We stumbled through the house, nearly falling over one another. We scrambled through the kitchen and out the back door.

The sky lit like a fireworks display. Fire blazed on top of the roof, cracking and hissing. Sparks rained down.

I snatched up Hugo, hugging him to me.

"Fire! Fire!" Betty yelled.

The "earthquake" Betty had unleashed on the neighborhood had folks dashing from their homes out onto the street.

"It's that dragon's fault," Betty yelled. "Get him out of here."

I decided to play this huge. I mean, I had a captive audience what with a third of the town in their pajamas staring at the house.

"Hugo didn't do anything. He's a baby!"

"Baby my toad-stooled butt," Betty said, throwing her weight from one hip to another. "That creature's dangerous. He needs to be locked up with the key thrown away. Lock him up, throw away the key and throw away the beast with it."

I clutched Hugo to me. "You monster. You've never liked him. From the first moment he hatched, all you saw was the evil, not the good. Maybe he was trying to save our lives from something and the house accidentally caught fire. Did you ever stop to think of that?"

"Yeah," Amelia yelled. "Little Hugo may've been trying to help us and you want to hang the little guy for doing us good."

Betty threw up her hands. "Will someone call the police? Only they can decide this."

Cordelia pointed to the house, which was smoking something fierce. "How about someone put out that fire first."

Betty shoved up her sleeves. "I have to do everything around here. I'm sick and tired of being the only person capable of fixing all the problems."

She clapped her hands. A thundercloud appeared over the roof and doused the flames. The fire hissed and sizzled as its life snuffed out.

"I'm going to put Hugo somewhere you can't hurt him," I said loudly.

"Oh yeah?" Betty said. "Where's that?"

"The front porch," I shouted, feeling stupid. This plan made no sense, but what the heck ever? I was going along with it all the way to the end. We were halfway to the finish line.

I strode into the house and out the front door. I tucked Hugo onto one of the rockers. "Stay right here, little guy, and try to look as inno-cent as you possibly can. I'm not sure if that's possible, but do your best."

I left and returned to the backyard, where the neighbors were helping Betty repair the roof. While everyone was talking and working magic, I sneaked inside.

At this point in the plan, if Betty's insane hypothesis was correct, someone would try to nab Hugo. If anyone watched the house to see if little Hugo had a moment to himself, this was the perfect chance to make a move.

I kept to the inside walls, creeping as stealthily as possible. I figured for this mission, Stealth was my middle name and not Clumsy-kins, which was probably more suitable since I'd never done a stakeout in my life.

I waited, listening for someone to hop on the porch and take Hugo. After several minutes of nothing happening, doubt crept in.

Really, this was a stupid plan. We were supposed to have a huge distraction in back, leave Hugo unattended and hope that if there was a dragon dealer around that they would snatch him up.

How stupid.

I'd done some cuckoo things since I'd been in Magnolia Cove. I'd hunted down a drunk naked mayor every morning, babysat a were-wolf, even started talking to animals, but this pretty much took the cake.

Setting up a baby dragon to be stolen was about as stupid is as stupid does.

And y'all, there wasn't even a box of chocolates involved.

I rose from my knees and decided that I'd grab Hugo and come inside.

Just then, a crash rattled the front porch.

I opened the front door and gasped.

Jennie the guard-vine lay broken on the floorboards. Her buds hung limply from the green winding stem. She'd been sheared right in half as if someone had walked up and cut her with a chainsaw.

Trust me, that's about what you'd have to use against her. That plant was practically made of steel.

But that wasn't the worst of it. Hugo stood in front of Jennie, his back arched, a growl rolling in his throat. He shot a stream of fire straight out front, toward the man who had a brown rope lassoed around the body of the little dragon.

"Axel," I said. "What are you doing?"

Axel's panicked gaze lifted to mine. There weren't any words he could say to explain what had happened.

Because I already understood.

His jailbird brother had tried to be a bad influence on Axel. Not long after mentioning that, Axel had broken up with me and had then asked if he could take Hugo—just for a while, he had said.

But he hadn't wanted him for a while, had he?

Axel had wanted him all along.

"Release him," I yelled. "Let Hugo go!"

Axel raised his palm. "Pepper, you don't understand."

Hugo shot out a stream of fire. A shield of magic flared from Axel's hand, stopping the flames from hurting him.

"Let him go, Axel."

"I'm trying to save him."

"That's not what it looks like."

"Someone else was here a moment ago. I stopped them. Pepper, you have to believe me."

"Then why's he attacking you?"

Axel's mouth pursed into a thin line but no words came.

"Release him," I demanded.

The rope around Hugo dissolved. The dragon didn't waste any time. It lunged for Axel.

Axel flared out his arms, stopping the beast mid-attack.

The way Hugo leaped toward Axel made my heart twist. No matter what, animal instincts were usually correct—even in a baby dragon that was only a few days old.

I hated to do it. I hated to believe Axel would try to take Hugo, but all the evidence pointed in that direction.

"You wanted him all along," I whispered.

Axel's face contorted in pain. "No, Pepper. Let me explain."

That's when anger fueled me. "What is there to explain? Axel, I want you gone. Don't ever show yourself here again."

Axel stared at me for a moment longer. His gaze flitted to the right as if he'd heard something. His eyes narrowed, then he flung out his arms and in a flash of light, vanished.

TWENTY

I carried Hugo into the house. Betty and my cousins rumbled in through the back door. Titters of laughter came from them, but when they saw me, everything stopped.

"What happened?" Cordelia said.

Amelia rushed over. She wrapped her arms around my shoulders. "You look like the whole world just collapsed beneath your feet."

My lips trembled as I set Hugo on the floor. I walked with wobbly knees over to the couch and sank onto it. I rubbed my temples.

"You're right. My whole world did just collapse."

"Did you catch 'em? Did we get the killer?"

"Worse than that," I said.

Betty pulled her corncob pipe from her pocket as if she was about to declare war. "What in tarnation could be worse than that?"

I grimaced. "Hugo was attacked. Jennie's been ripped in half. But the worst of it is that Axel attacked Hugo. At least, that's what it looked like."

Betty grabbed her face with her hands. "Jennie's been attacked!"

Right. Out of all this, that was the most important thing. Not the fact that my heart was crushed and lying bleeding on the floor. It had been bad enough that Axel wanted to cool things off for a while. I figured we'd get back together. There's undeniable chemistry between us. Enough to make me want to sit in his lap and purr.

But obviously, now all that was over.

Betty rushed through the living room and threw open the door. We followed her out onto the porch where she pulled Jennie into her palms. The buds sagged limply.

"I'm not sure if I can save her, but I'll try. This flower has been in my family since the turn of the century. If anyone could survive a meteor falling to earth or the zombie apocalypse you kids think is going to happen one day, it would be Jennie."

Betty cracked her knuckles and rubbed her hands together as if warming them. A flicker of magic ignited on her fingertips. A golden thread coiled and rotated from Betty's trimmed nails.

The yarn wound around Jennie. A halo of light pulsed from the thread as Jennie the guard-vine wove together. The string coiled around and around, stitching every bud and every leaf to each stem.

"Girls, help me get her into place."

We each gathered part of the vine and hooked her above the porch. The golden halo hummed on my fingers. I wondered if the healing energy throbbing in the vine could ease the pain that was slowly shredding my heart in two.

Betty clapped her hands and the magic snapped off. The golden thread dissolved, raining on the floor like the ends of a lit sparkler a child holds on the fourth of July.

Jennie's color deepened, her buds swelled and the green vine returned to its lush color.

"I think she'll be just fine," Betty said.

"Yes, she looks like she'll do great. It's a good thing we came along when we did," Amelia said. "But I worry that our Pepper is not going to be okay."

I forced a feeble smile to my lips. "I'll be fine, y'all. Really."

Betty huffed. "You will not *be fine*. You will tell us everything that happened and then we will decide as a family who's going to be fine and who isn't."

Um. Okay.

I rubbed my forehead. "Can I have some sweet tea?"

Betty glanced up and down the street. "That sounds like good idea. Let's get inside."

I staggered in and sat by the hearth. Betty pointed a finger and the fire crackled and spat to life. She clapped her hands and a service of sweet tea appeared. She poured a glass and slid it through the air to me.

I caught it and drank deeply. Sweet sugary nectar slipped down my throat. I grabbed a handful of jellybeans from my pocket and dropped them in. I let them dissolve for a moment and then sipped again.

Better.

Betty stirred the fire. "Now. Tell us what happened."

"I heard a racket and ran to the porch. When I got there, I found Axel with a rope tied around Hugo, and the Hugo attacking Axel."

"What?" Amelia said. "I don't understand."

I rubbed a line of sweat from the glass. "I didn't tell y'all this, but a couple of days ago Axel admitted that his brother recently escaped from prison."

"No," Amelia said.

"Right. He also said his brother was involved with some sort of illegal dealings, obviously, which is what sent him to prison. But Adam had also tried to get Axel to turn to the dark side, so to speak. Then Axel broke up with me."

"What? He broke up with you?" Amelia said.

"Would you stop saying 'what' and just listen," Cordelia said.

"Okay," Amelia whimpered.

"Yeah, but that's not the worst of it. The other day I saw Axel and he suggested that he take Hugo off my hands."

Betty and my cousins exchanged raised eyebrows.

I rubbed my temples. "I know. It looks bad. And then I catch him roping Hugo. When I asked why, he said someone else had just been there, but y'all, then Hugo shot fire at Axel. The dragon clearly attacked him."

I exhaled. "And I hate to say it, but why would Hugo have spat fire at Axel if Axel wasn't trying to do something bad?"

Amelia's brows wrinkled. "Axel, a dragon stealer? I don't see it."

Cordelia shook her head. "I wouldn't think the man so many of us have protected would turn around and do that."

Betty stroked her chin. "He gets steady work as a private investigator. I don't see why he'd need to do that." She flicked her hand. "But more important, does his character reveal him to be the sort of person who would sell magical creatures? He's a magical creature himself. Though there are always stories of folks turning on their own kind, I doubt he's that sort. He's got too high a standard to be someone who would do that. At least, that's how it seemed." She gave me a pointed look. "But what do you think?"

I shook my head. "But I just don't understand. I can't believe I'd be so mistaken about Axel, y'all. He's one of the good guys—or so I thought." I rubbed at a spot pounding in my forehead. "I don't know."

So many conflicting thoughts and statements. *Axel was a good guy. He wouldn't do this.* Everything in my body screamed that was true, but I couldn't just ignore what I had seen and how Hugo had reacted. There was something there. Something I didn't understand—but Hugo had.

"If it makes you feel any better, we could spy on Axel," Amelia said.

I grimaced. "I hate to do that."

"How else are you going to know the truth?"

Cordelia glared at Amelia. "She could trust Axel and see how it plays out." She glanced at me. "There's something in my gut that says Axel is innocent. I know the dragon works on a different level than we do, and I'm sure he had a reason for attacking Axel, but I can't believe that it was because Axel attacked the dragon."

"I don't know," I said uneasily. "Axel had him in a rope."

"You could talk to him about it," Cordelia said.

"I did. It didn't get me anywhere."

Everyone was silent. The air seemed to thicken, fill with the uncomfortable truth surrounding us.

"At this point," I said boldly, "Axel can't be trusted. Not until we discover the truth. He's helped us several times, but I am charged with keeping all the animals under my care safe and sound. Not only that, if Uncle Donovan sent Hugo to be my protector then I have to do everything I can to bond with this dragon and not betray him. I won't put him in a situation where he can be hurt. I just won't."

"Axel's never done anything wrong," Betty said. "But I understand where you're coming from. Everyone under this roof will abide by your decision."

She snapped her fingers and shots of honeysuckle wine floated in front of us. Betty circled her fingers around the glass and lifted it in the air.

"The four of us witches will keep this dragon and you, Pepper, safe. If that means our friends are now our enemies, then that's the way it's supposed to be. Until such time as we have proof that Axel Reign is innocent, he is no longer on our list of friends."

"Is that a written list I'm not aware of?" Amelia said. "Because I may need to take a look at it and make sure I'm up to date on who's who."

Cordelia elbowed her. "It's not written. It's an understood list."

"Oh, okay," she said.

"Are all of my girls with me?" Betty said.

Amelia frowned, but lifted her glass. Cordelia's face twisted into a sour expression. I guessed her insides felt about as dour as she looked. But still, my cousin raised her arm with the glass.

It was my turn.

A wave of nausea flooded my stomach. I held it in, putting the pieces of the puzzle together. They didn't lock, but I knew eventually they would and until that time it was better to be safe than sorry.

"From now on," I said, "until the time that he's proven innocent, Axel Reign is no longer my friend. He is my enemy."

TWENTY-ONE

By the time I carried Hugo upstairs, the dragon was asleep in my arms. I told Mattie, who was resting on my bed, what had happened.

"Hmm, seems odd, sugar," she said, stretching.

"I know. There's something not right about it, or maybe I just don't want it to be right. Perhaps that's the problem. I feel like a fly stuck in sugar water. I can't stop drinking but I need to get out before I drown. I know Axel enough to say it doesn't seem likely, but there it is splashed out in front of me."

"What? Some evidence?"

"Pretty much."

"I cain't say I can help you," Mattie said. "I am, after all, just a cat. My experience in all this human stuff is limited."

I smiled sadly. "I know."

I changed into my pajamas and slid under the covers. "It seems like a terrible nightmare. Maybe when I wake up in the morning I'll find that it was a dream, and the Axel I know is still the same man he was yesterday, but now he wants to date me."

"You got the love feelings for him, huh?" Mattie said.

I choked. "What? Love? No. I've known him a month or so. Not love. But it's a serious case of like, that's for sure. Enough that my heart hurts knowing that he'd betray us. Animal-parts dealing? I just can't believe it."

Mattie yawned. "It might be like you said. Maybe when you wake up everything will make sense."

"I hope so."

I didn't sleep well that night. I tossed and turned, punched my pillow and even flipped it over to the cool side about a thousand times. But rest evaded me. The only thing I had was a whirling, churning mind that offered no answers, only more questions.

Questions I needed to know the answers to. The first place to start was back at Hattie Hollypop's. If anyone was involved, it was her. That much, I was positive of.

Well, almost positive.

But I had a serious inkling that she might be able to help.

ON WEDNESDAY, I made it to Brews and Jewels a little after it opened. I convinced Betty to watch the pet shop, but informed her that the first animals she was to guide patrons to were kittens, puppies and birds. She was not to sell the iguanas as first-line familiars.

And I thought that would've been common sense.

Anyway, Hattie smiled widely when she saw me. "Good morning."

"'Morning," I said. I pulled the ripped sheet from my purse and smoothed it on the counter.

"This again?" she said.

"Yeah, you know I was thinking...and I'm not saying anything is wrong with the bloodstone that you used. Not in the least. In fact, I'm sure it's incredibly powerful. But I got to thinking. What if—and this is a big *what if*. But what if your bloodstone is a bit too old to work well?"

Hattie laughed. "Impossible. The age of such magic has nothing to do with its power."

I quirked what I hoped was an intimidating eyebrow. "Really? Are you sure about that? Because I was talking to my grandmother, Betty Craple—I'm sure you know her. Betty was telling me that over time a magical amulet could lose its power. It's not unheard of, she said. And if there's a witch I'm willing to believe, it's her."

Hattie's face reddened. She gritted her teeth. "I promise you there's nothing wrong with my stone."

I shrugged, playing up the whole innocent role thing. "But how can you be sure? I mean, really? How can you know that? I just don't understand."

Hattie's lips pinched. "Because I know."

I leaned forward. "But how can you know *for sure?*"

"Because that bloodstone isn't old."

I tipped my head back. "It's not? But I would've thought something like that was thousands of years old, passed from generation to generation."

Hattie's jaw clenched. "What I'm about to tell you can't be repeated to anybody."

"Never."

I crossed my fingers behind my back. I hated lying, but this was information I had to know. If breaking a small promise brought me some answers, then so be it.

"I'm only saying it to uphold the reputation of my shop."

"Of course."

Hattie's gaze darted from side to side to make sure no one else was listening. "That stone isn't thousands of years old."

I gasped and clutched the imaginary pearls hanging around my neck. "It's not?"

"No. That bloodstone was fresh."

"Fresh? What do you mean?"

"I mean I have a supplier. Dragon bloodstone is popular so I found someone who could supply what I needed."

I glared at her. "Are you saying you buy dragons?"

She shook her head. "No. I'm not saying that at all. I don't buy dragons, only the after products. But I do know a person who trades in bloodstones."

I smiled, knowing what was coming. This would be Mysterio of course. It would be him. He would be whom Hattie pointed to.

"Who?" I whispered. "Who would trade in such a thing?"

"I shouldn't tell you."

Of course, you should!

"Oh, I won't say anything."

"It's just that you're acquainted with him."

Dread filled the pit of my stomach. She would say it was Axel. Dear Lord, it was true. He tried to kill Hugo for some sort of illegal bloodstone trade. I might faint.

"Barry the Dragon Tamer."

I choked. "What?"

Hattie nodded. "That's right. Barry the Dragon Tamer is who sold me the stones. Now, where he gets his dragons, I don't know."

I thanked Hattie for her time. I laughed bitterly. She didn't have to tell me who Barry bought his dragons from. I already knew.

He bought them from Mysterio.

I walked toward the shop lost in my thoughts. I stared at the ground, trying to figure out a way to get what we needed. If Barry was the bloodstone dealer and he got his supply from Mysterio, how was Axel involved? Was he a second dealer? And was he connected to Barry as well?

All these thoughts swirled in my head until I collided with a massive chest.

"Sorry," I said, glancing up and locking eyes with Axel.

"Sorry," he murmured as he strode past.

What the heck? Was that it? No "hello"? No "sorry I tried to steal your dragon"? No nothing? Who the heck did Axel Reign think he was?

I looked over my shoulder, watching as he kept right on walking down the street. Axel didn't bother to look back.

Well, if he wasn't going to look back, then I wasn't either.

From this moment on, I was only looking forward.

~

I GOT home that evening and sat at the dinner table in silence. Well, I was the one being silent, not everyone else.

Betty chewed the end of her fried pork chop. "What's going on, Pepper?"

I sighed, nearly sinking my face into the baked macaroni and cheese that took up half my plate. "I went to Hattie Hollypop's today. She said that Barry the one and only Dragon Tamer sells dragon bloodstones."

Betty gasped. "Not Barry."

I smirked. "Are you sure he's even legit? Who has a name like Barry?"

"Barry does," Betty said.

"You know what I mean." I jabbed a macaroni with my fork and popped it in my mouth. "Anyway, Barry's the one doing the selling."

Betty stroked her chin. "Then we need someone to do some buying."

Amelia blinked widely. "Who?"

"You," Betty said.

Cordelia choked back a laugh. "You think anyone would believe that Amelia wants to buy a bloodstone? It makes more sense for Pepper to try to sell Hugo to Barry and then we follow Barry to see what he does with the dragon."

"That may put Hugo in danger," I said.

Betty nodded. "I agree. The best thing to do is have Pepper try to buy a bloodstone from Barry and if Barry doesn't bite, have Pepper try to sell Hugo for his own safety."

"That's what I just said," Cordelia grumbled.

"I know. I thought if we heard it twice y'all might be more likely to go for it."

"I don't know," I said. "Barry might disappear and then we'd lose Hugo forever."

Betty smacked her lips. "Not if he knows what you want going into it. If Barry knows you're going to sell Hugo he may have the whole scheme lined up. What I'm saying is whoever does some of the other handling could be nearby. I can promise you that Barry is not the one getting his hands dirty. He's got too much to lose with his show. Barry is going to hand the dragon off to someone else. From there, we follow and see what happens. I think that's our best plan."

What if Barry handed Hugo off to Axel?

Either way, that's what I had to know. I needed the truth. The truth would set me free, as they say. I wouldn't have to worry or wonder anymore. I'd know exactly what was happening.

"Should we contact Garrick?" Cordelia asked.

Betty shook her head. "No. No reason to tip off the police. It might be nothing, though I bet it's something. I'll have their number on standby in case we get in trouble and have to call."

Amelia jabbed a piece of pork with her knife. "My guess is we'll find ourselves in trouble. That's how these things always seem to go."

I shrugged. "Maybe not. Maybe we'll be fine." I dabbed my napkin over my lips and said, "Okay. What's the first thing we do?"

Betty's eyes sparkled as she said, "First thing we need to do is set a trap. Pepper, get on the phone to Barry. Make the call and we'll take it from there."

I cringed. "But wait. If Axel is in on this, then won't Barry tell him? That'll blow everything because Axel knows we suspect him."

Betty twisted her face until it looked like she was suffering from a serious bout of constipation. "Don't worry about Axel. I'll put a bug in town that you want to get rid of the dragon and not have to worry about him anymore. If Axel gets wind of it, he'll be less likely to be suspicious."

"How's that?" I said.

"I'll make sure it comes from the police. That way Axel won't suspect anything."

I rolled my eyes. "Right. He is pretty smart."

Betty smirked. "You just call Barry. That's the first thing we need to do."

"When?"

"Now."

"Now?" I nearly screamed. "I'm not prepared. Not emotionally ready to take this on."

"Well get ready because we need you front and center of this thing."

I exhaled. "Fine. I'll make the call. But when are you going to handle Axel?"

Betty shuffled from her chair and started upstairs. "In a little while. Trust me on this. Do your part and Axel won't be a problem."

I shot Cordelia and Amelia concerned looks. They both shrugged.

"Since everyone seems to be in agreement, I'll do it."

Betty disappeared up the stairs. I heaped a spoonful of banana pudding onto my plate. "But not until I have some dessert first."

I called Barry as soon as Betty had reappeared from her room, having done whatever mysteries of the universe she had to perform.

I found a quiet spot and dialed.

"Hello?"

"Um, Hi, Barry. This is Pepper Dunn."

"Oh, hi Pepper."

Long pause. Nerves flittered about my stomach. "I hope I'm not bothering you."

"No bother at all."

"We had a situation last night. Hugo set fire to the house."

"Oh no," Barry said.

"Yeah, it wasn't good. Betty's threatening to get rid of Hugo, but I don't want to abandon him. I want him with someone who cares about dragons and who will take excellent care of him."

"Of course."

I sighed. "You see, he's grown on me and I just hate to think of giving him to the wrong person. I know you've got your show and all, and I hate to burden you, but I was wondering if maybe you knew someone who could help? Someone who wouldn't mind having him? I don't want money."

Short pause. "I can take him."

"You can? I hate for him to be an inconvenience."

"It's not an inconvenience. I've been looking for a new dragon. Some of mine, though royal as they may be, are getting old and need to be replaced. I have no problem taking Hugo."

I pretended to stifle a sob. "Can you take him tomorrow morning? I hate for it to be such a rush, but Betty's been pretty erratic. I don't know if she'll let him stay much longer."

"I can meet then."

"Great."

We agreed to meet in the same park where we'd worked with Hugo before. As I hung up the phone, the nervous pit in my stomach grew.

This would either go exactly right, or it would go very, very wrong.

I crossed my fingers that it would go right because there was less than twelve hours between me and go time.

TWENTY-TWO

I arrived at the park early—like an hour early. Cordelia and Amelia were set up around the perimeter. They had walkie-talkies to keep in contact with each other and Betty. Betty had managed to snag some sort of wire with a mic and speaker that snaked up my back and clipped to my t-shirt.

"Why aren't we using magic?" I said.

"Sometimes man-made things are easier," Betty replied. "Besides, if one of y'all gets scared, I can't rely on you to use your magic correctly to communicate."

"Thanks," Amelia said pertly. "I appreciate the compliment."

"Not a compliment," I said.

"Where'd you get all this high-tech gear?" Cordelia had asked.

"I keep things," was all Betty said.

"And we won't have to worry about Axel blowing this?" I said.

Betty slid a finger over her nose. "No. We don't have to worry about him."

"Okay," I said.

We got into place and I decided to spend a little time playing catch with Hugo. I tossed a ball and he flew after it, diving and turning in the air. His acrobatics made my heart soar.

We got into a good rhythm—I threw, he fetched to the point where I knew when he would ascend and then dive. It was almost as if I were in his mind. The connection linking us was so strong that I started talking.

"Soar."

He would rise.

"Dive."

He was fall.

"Shoot fire."

Girlfriend, dragon spat a flame.

I jumped. "Holy shrimp and grits. So this is it. This is the connection."

I felt it in my heart that Hugo was supposed to be mine, so when Barry appeared in the distance, I started feeling all Mother Bear, ready for a fight to the finish to see who would become the little dragon's owner.

"Come," I said to Hugo.

The dragon drifted down, beating his wings until he settled on my shoulders.

"You're early," Barry said.

"Yeah. Betty was a tyrant last night. She was just awful. I slipped out early this morning, trying to get time with Hugo. He's such a sweet dragon."

Barry patted Hugo's head. "Yeah. He's going to be great in Witch Vegas. Seriously. He's got the exact right temperament to train for shows."

"I'm sure going to miss him," I said.

Barry smiled. "You can visit whenever you'd like."

"Thanks," I said.

I uncoiled Hugo from my shoulders and squeezed him tight before handing him to Barry. "Let me know when you're settled in. I'd like to see him."

Barry hugged Hugo to him. "Will do."

He walked off toward the woods. I waited for Betty to give me the signal.

My heart pounded. My breath hitched. Betty was closest to where Barry had come from. She would have watched him pull up.

I squeezed the button on my communicator. "Betty, what's the word?"

Static filled the air until I finally heard a crackle. "A truck's pulling up to where Barry is. Looks like we were right. As soon as he had Hugo, Barry was going to do a deal."

"What are we waiting for? Come on," I said.

I ran toward the woods, breaking branches and snapping twigs as I rushed over the grass. I saw two vehicles up ahead.

And I saw two men—Barry holding Hugo and Axel preparing to take the dragon from him.

"Everyone stop! Police!"

Suddenly, Garrick Young and company stormed into the woods. The police, looking like extras from the cast of *Van Helsing*, surrounded the two men, raining down order on them.

Axel's face twisted with fury. Before he could take hold of Hugo, he clapped his hands and disappeared.

I crumpled to the ground as police swept past me, grabbing Barry and forcing his hands behind his back.

"Don't move," Garrick said. "You're under arrest."

As he started to read Barry his rights, the Dragon Tamer screamed that he was innocent. That he hadn't done anything wrong.

I stared at the scene, totally confused. My head swam from disbelief. Everything seemed to move in super slow motion.

I didn't register anything until I felt a hand on my shoulder. I glanced up to see Betty wearing thick black glasses and smoking her corncob pipe.

"Looks like we got the villain," she said.

Then why do I feel so bad?

TWENTY-THREE

"Mr. Dragon Tamer says you asked him to take care of Hugo."

"Is that his real last name?" I said. "Dragon Tamer?"

I sat in Garrick's office. Betty sat beside me. I suppose she'd come along for moral support, or simply to make sure things went the way we needed them to go.

My stomach was so knotted I wasn't sure which way that was.

"Yep," Garrick said, beating his thumbs on the armrests of his chair. "Says that you wanted him to take the dragon." He opened a manila folder. "But if this guy is who we think he is, he's been grinding up dragons for quite a while and selling them on the black market."

I grimaced. "Thanks for the image."

Garrick pinched the brim of his hat and ran his fingers along the line. "Dragon Tamer swears he was handing the creature off to someone else who wanted to buy it from him."

"And how did someone else know to contact him?"

"*Been* in contact with him," he said.

I pushed up. "But that's not what Hattie Hollypop said. She said that Barry was a well-known dragon bloodstone dealer. That's where she'd gotten hers from."

"Yep," Garrick said. "Barry confessed to selling stones, but said he got them from Mysterio."

I clicked my tongue. "So they were in on it together. Mysterio was buying up dragons and then turning over the stones to Barry to sell."

"But that's as far as it ever went with Barry," Garrick said. "He would sell some, but he swears he never had more than a few to sell at any one time."

I sank into the chair. "So where does this put us? What about Axel?"

Garrick's mouth tightened. "I've been unable to reach Mr. Reign."

I cracked my knuckles and raked my fingers through my hair. "So basically we're nowhere."

Garrick shot me a knowing look. "I'm still investigating. I don't know what y'all ladies are doing running around in a forest with walkie-talkies and setting up dragon purchase deals, but my suggestion is to leave this sort of thing to the professionals. Let me investigate and if you want to sell a baby dragon, I think you should sell him from your own shop *legally*—not in the backwoods."

Heat flushed my face. "Okay, officer. You're right."

Betty rose. "Come on, Pepper. Let's go."

We walked out of the station. "So what does any of this mean?" I said.

"It means we got the wrong man," Betty grumbled.

"And it also means Garrick said to stay out of it," I said. "Probably for the best. It's all a bunch of random events. Besides, I'll never know what my mother wanted to tell me anyway."

Betty fisted a hand on her hip. "I've been telling you what she wanted you to know—she loves you. Would you stop asking about it? There were three things in life your mother loved—the smell of gardenias, your father and you. Four—me, as well."

Properly chastened, I hanged my head. "All right. But I still feel like this whole thing was a bust. Axel's clearly involved. Barry was selling.

Mysterio was buying up dragons. But we still don't understand why Mysterio was murdered. Not that any of it matters."

"Because your heart hurts," Betty said.

"Yeah."

She wrapped a grandmotherly arm around my shoulders. "Everything will turn out all right in the end. It always does."

I forced a smile. "I'm sure you're right."

I followed her to the house, where Cordelia and Amelia had changed out of their green and brown and into normal clothes. "Well, that was all in a good day's work, don't you y'all think?" Amelia said.

I shrugged. "I suppose."

Cordelia and Amelia exchanged glances. "Are you opening your store today?"

I shook my head. "No. I've closed due to special circumstances."

Cordelia flipped a strand of hair over her shoulder. "Why don't you come with us? We're going out for ice cream and shopping."

A genuine smile tugged on my lips. "Will there be banana splits involved?"

Amelia fingered her pixie cut hair. "You bet. And I'm sure we can manage to throw some jelly beans on top."

I laughed. "Okay. That sounds great."

We left, but not before I gave Hugo a pat on the head. Betty promised to take good care of him and my cousins and I set off for Marshmallow Magic, my cousin Carmen's store.

Carmen sold all sorts of sweets and she even had an ice cream counter where she scooped up sundaes, shakes and cones, along with molded chocolate bats and hard sugar-candy frogs.

Everything was delicious.

I ordered a sundae with chocolate sauce, marshmallow topping and of course, cinnamon jelly beans.

We sat at a booth. I licked my lips as I eyed my concoction.

"That looks heavenly," Amelia said.

I moaned as the marshmallow and cinnamon hit my tongue and slid down my throat. "It is. Want a bite?"

"Yes," she said, giggling.

We exchanged bites of our treats until we were so stuffed and exhausted from the sugar rush that each of us sprawled on our seats.

"Do y'all feel up for shopping?" Cordelia said. "Or would y'all rather hang out here and melt into the cushions?"

I laughed, pushing up. "I'm ready for some retail therapy. Where are we going?"

"I was thinking Witch's Wardrobe. I saw a pair of web earrings I want."

"Oh?" Amelia said. "Do you need them for a date?"

Cordelia raked her fingers through her hair. "Okay, fine. I guess it's time for me to finally fess up."

"We've been waiting for you to do that," I said. "I can't wait to hear all the details."

Cordelia rolled her eyes. "Zach and I broke up three weeks ago."

"What?" I said. "You never told us."

"I didn't want to give Betty the satisfaction of knowing. She's never liked the fact that Zach and I were long distance, so I kept up the pretense. Then I met someone."

"Garrick," I said.

She glared at me. "Yes, Garrick."

"You don't have to hide it from us," Amelia said. "We like Garrick and we trust your instincts."

Cordelia's shoulders relaxed. "I was afraid y'all would judge me. Garrick and I are going slow, but I really like him."

I grinned. "I like him, too."

Cordelia smiled. "Good...Now, let's go get some spider web earrings."

We went to the house and picked up our cast iron skillets to fly over to Witch's Wardrobe.

It was mid-afternoon. The sun suspended high in the sky. We landed near the clothing store. Gretchen Gargoyle greeted us when we entered..

Cordelia went straight to the earrings and I walked around while Amelia perused the cobweb undergarments.

I found a bright blue tunic that I figured would look great with my red hair and might not make the freckles on my nose stand out too much. I slipped into a dressing room and changed. The dress felt good, but I wanted a second opinion. I exited the room.

Gretchen met me outside. "That looks great, Pepper. Though it needs some accessories. I think I've got a belt that would look perfect. Just came in. I haven't even put them out. Follow me, sister, and I'll get you squared away."

Her excitement had me curious. I followed Gretchen to her office.

"Darn, they must be in the storeroom. I thought I'd left them in here. I'll be right back."

"Pepper," Amelia called out.

"Yes," I answered.

Amelia and Cordelia popped into the office.

Amelia ran her fingers over her pixie cut. "If you're going to be a few minutes the two of us are going to step over to Spellin' Skillet and grab some supper so that Betty doesn't have to cook."

I glanced at Cordelia. "Did you already pay for the earrings?"

She raised a bag in reply.

"Okay. I'll be here."

They disappeared and I took a minute to glance around the office. On the table lay an ashtray with half a cigar snubbed out in it.

I peered closer. It looked like the exact same type of cigar I'd seen in Mysterio's room at the inn.

But Mysterio didn't smoke.

Then who did the cigar belong to?

My gaze drifted to the opposite side of the desk. On the corner sat an open box with plastic bubble packaging overflowing from the lid.

"Are these the belts?"

I peeled back the cover expecting to see belts, but instead I found stones. Dark blood-colored rocks.

My fingers numbed. My jaw dropped as the pieces of the puzzle finally fit together.

The cigar I found in Mysterio's room. Axel had said his brother smoked, that he had traded illegal objects, but Axel hadn't said what kind. Then there was the fact that Axel hadn't seemed to recognize me at the police station or out on the street when we bumped into each other.

My fingers were still on the box when I heard Gretchen re-enter.

"Well, well, well, I was hoping you wouldn't look in there."

I turned and saw Gretchen in the doorway. She pulled a gun from her pocket and pointed it at me.

My heart thundered. "What are you going to do with me?"

"Why, kill you, of course."

TWENTY-FOUR

J stared at the gun leveled at my chest. You know, it never failed to surprise me that witches that used magic in their everyday lives relied on guns to kill people.

It was something I didn't understand.

"So you got rid of Mysterio," I said.

Gretchen smirked. "Figured it out a little too late, didn't you?"

"Better late than never, they always say."

Gretchen rested her gun hand on her other arm as if to stabilize herself. "We were partners for years. Mysterio purchased the dragons and I took care of the other side—the dirty work, so they say. But Mysterio got greedy. He wanted to cut me out of our deals. Yes, he loved to have affairs with women. None of that bothered me. I didn't care. All I wanted was the money."

She backed up and jerked her hand for me to exit the room. "I'm not going to shoot you in my office. Too big a chance of bloodying up the carpet. I want you to head to the sales floor. The linoleum will be better for clean up."

How thoughtful of her.

I shuffled to the front. Gretchen snapped her fingers. A CLOSED sign swung into place and large black drapes shuttered the windows.

"My cousins will be right back," I said.

She smirked. "By that time you'll have disappeared. I'll pretend not to know where you've gone."

I hated it when killers had decent plans. "Then what happened? Mysterio double cross you? You might as well tell me before you kill me."

"He cut me out of several deals and I discovered he was going to desert me completely. I couldn't have that. I make too much money from the stones," Gretchen snapped. "So I concocted a plan."

Just then, a figure emerged from the back. He looked exactly like Axel but I could see a small tattoo peeking out from above the top button of his shirt.

"Adam Reign, I presume," I said.

He smirked.

"How'd you figure that out?" Gretchen asked.

"The cigars. Found one in Mysterio's room and another in your office."

Gretchen shot him a scathing look. "I told you to clean those up."

"No big deal," he said.

"I thought you were your brother," I said. "He didn't tell me he had a twin."

Adam smiled. "I'm the better looking one, I think."

Though he did look almost identical to Axel, there was something just a little rough around the edges about him. It wasn't something I would have noticed if I didn't know that they were twins, as I'd mistaken Adam for Axel a couple of times already.

I turned back to Gretchen. "What kind of plan did you concoct against Mysterio?"

With the gun pointed at me, she confessed. "That night, Adam went up to Mysterio's room to ask questions about who to buy stones from. Mysterio happened to write my address on a paper."

Adam agreed. "I ripped it off and spelled the cape using a potion Gretchen had made."

"But why didn't Mysterio sell you the stones himself? If he was cutting you out of deals, Gretchen, wouldn't Mysterio have wanted to sell to Adam?"

"He was acting nervous," Adam said.

The potion. The one that Betty had spelled Hugo with probably made Mysterio a nervous wreck. After all, when we saw him right before he died, he nearly threw the cage at us as if it was on fire.

"It didn't matter if Mysterio sold Adam the stones or not. The point was to get close enough to him to spell his cape," Gretchen said.

She smiled. "Even though I wasn't the original designer, I know a trick or two to make clothing do what I want. I knew that the cops would suspect me because of my relationship with Mysterio and my talents with fabric, so I dragged out those old letters to point to Idie Claire Hawker. It was simple and easy."

"And then you discovered I had a dragon and wanted him for yourself."

Gretchen's face twisted into a sick grin. It sent a shudder through me. "You know what's funny? I didn't even know about your dragon until that day you came into my shop with it around your neck. I told Idie Claire that Hattie attended Sunday yoga because I figured you'd need her bloodstones, given the ripped off note you'd found that held part of your mother's message. You made a big enough deal about it that I knew Hattie would be someone that could help you decipher it.

"So that's how we all ended up at yoga. I figured if I made your dragon seem dangerous enough, you'd either decide to sell him or we'd steal him. I cast a spell that made a little bit of his inner dragon come out against the cats and dogs. I figured if he was a public nuisance you'd be more willing to get rid of him."

"So you watched the house," I said. My gaze bobbed around the room. I was looking for a chance to escape, but with Gretchen and Adam in the store, my chances of dashing were slim.

"And we almost had him," Gretchen said.

My gaze shifted to Adam. "But he torched you."

"Sneaky little dragon," he spat. "He attacked me hard enough that I ran off."

"But not before Axel showed up." I put all of that together. "The dragon was in such a fury that he then turned to Axel while you escaped. Scared of a baby dragon, are you?"

Adam crossed his massive prison-workout arms across his chest. "Once you go missing, it'll be easier to swoop in and steal him."

"There's no way I'm going to let that happen."

The voice shot out from behind Gretchen. Both criminals whirled around. Standing in the hallway, a halo of light glowing around him from the open office door, stood Axel.

I almost dropped to my knees in thanks.

Axel stepped closer. His gaze flickered from his doppelgänger to me. "I see you've met my twin brother, Adam. He met Gretchen in prison and I believe she helped him escape."

"What can I say?" Gretchen said. "Wickedness is fun."

Axel studied his brother. "Lot of people looking for you. That was pretty brave, showing up at the police station pretending to be me to find out what the word on street was about your own release."

"I'm nothing if not resourceful, brother," Adam said. "You could've joined me. We'd have made such a great pair."

I fisted my hands to my hips. "Okay, enough with the reunion crap. Axel, why the heck didn't you tell me you had a twin? Don't you think that would've kept me from totally wigging out on you the other night if you'd admitted Hugo had attacked Adam?"

He made a soothing motion. "I didn't want Adam to know we were on to him."

"You let me think you attacked my dragon!"

"I needed you to believe it was me."

"Why?"

He sighed. "So I could track Adam down. Listen, can we talk about this later, when you don't have a gun pointed at you?"

I shook my head. "No. I'd like an explanation now."

"If you don't shut up, I'm going to shoot you both," Gretchen said.

I clamped my mouth, but I glared at Axel. He should've told that Adam was his twin. I mean honestly, it would've saved a ton of heartache on my end.

"Shoot me," Axel said. "Leave her alone."

Gretchen glanced at Adam. "Take him."

In that moment, Gretchen flicked the gun off me.

I took a chance and lunged. At the same time, Axel shot out a stream of magic that coiled around Adam.

Adam flexed his chest, and in an instant, the inner beast started breaking free. Hair sprouted on his chest, his and arms face elongated. My gaze flickered to Axel, who was shifting as well.

Both men were turning into werewolves.

I didn't know if it was because of Adam that Axel was changing, because he couldn't shift on his own will. He'd said it only happened at the full moon.

But there was no time to ponder it.

My arm collided with Gretchen's elbow. A gunshot rang out in the room. The bullet hit the glass, shattering a window. The weapon flew from Gretchen's hand, clattering across the floor. She cocked her arm as if to punch me.

I dodged, falling to the ground and grabbing her ankles. I pulled until she fell on her rump.

Nearby, both men, still partially changed, were locked combat.

Gretchen scrambled for the gun. I tugged her back. Her foot collided with the side of my head. I shook off the pain and pushed up to my feet.

I threw myself on Gretchen.

"Get off," she yelled, thrashing around.

I wedged an elbow into her back. She howled in pain.

At the same time, one of the half-wolves threw the other across the room and raised his hand.

A stream of magic shot out, coiling around the opposite beast. I held my breath as the beast shifted back to his human form.

It was Adam.

I exhaled.

Axel, now changing back, unleashed another stream of magic on Gretchen.

"I can't move," she said hoarsely. I dug my elbow a little farther in her back just for good measure.

"It's about time," I said.

With both suspects subdued, I glanced at Axel, who was now himself completely. "Wow, you are some wizard."

His lips curved into a smile so delicious I wanted to lick it. Yes, lick it.

"All that matters is that you're safe," he said.

My heart melted a little as the sound of sirens filled the afternoon air.

TWENTY-FIVE

We sat outside, waiting for Garrick and his crew to finish arresting Gretchen and Adam, who was clearly going back to prison.

My cousins had shown up and had been in total shock once I explained what happened. I shooed them on home with supper and told them I'd be back later.

I pulled a blanket over my shoulders. The wool scratched my skin, and the thick material made me glad that fabric softener existed and that I used it. "So *why* exactly couldn't you tell me what was going on?"

Axel exhaled a deep shot of air. Trouble darkened his blue eyes. He held my gaze with a look that stole my breath not only from my lungs, but all the way from the bottom of my toes.

"There was a manhunt for Adam, but he was staying hidden. With his past dealings in illegal objects, I had an idea he might somehow be involved. But Adam is smart and evasive. I couldn't track him down. Neither could Garrick. But I knew he'd eventually show up, once I figured out who was the person behind Mysterio's death."

"I'm not buying it."

"I figured Adam was involved once you mentioned finding the

cigar in Mysterio's room. Cigars were always his favorite. But I didn't know who he was working with. At first, it looked like it was going to be Barry the Dragon Tamer, but it wasn't. If Adam had known I was on to him, he would've stayed far away from Gretchen. I just planned on asking her some questions when I found you."

I sighed, pulling the blanket tighter across my shoulders. "But you let me think that you were involved. You don't know what that did to me. It was horrible. Awful. I felt like I didn't know who you are."

He cringed. "I'm sorry. If I had to do it over, I would've let you know."

"Did Betty?"

"Yes. But she already knew about Adam; she was only keeping up pretenses because she knew I'd want her to."

"Well aren't you two peas in a pod."

"I was hoping more like you and me in a pod instead of me and an old lady."

I edged away. "You broke up with me.."

Axel raked his fingers through his hair. "To keep you safe. You might not believe this, but every choice I made, I did for your protection. Pepper, I may not have known you long, but I know what you are in my heart. You're important. Not just to me, but to this entire town. Trust me. I don't like keeping secrets from people—"

"—You keep a lot," I interrupted.

"For other's safety," he insisted. "Putting distance between us kept Adam away from you. He wanted Hugo, not you and I wanted to make sure it stayed that way. Otherwise..." He raked his fingers through his hair. "Otherwise, Adam might've shifted his focus to capturing you—just to get to me. I couldn't have that."

He grabbed my hand and kissed my palm. Shivers shot right to my heart.

"All this time I kept tabs on you, made sure you were okay. I'm not the sort of man who walks into a woman's life lightly. I tread a dark, dangerous path because of what I am. I try to keep it separate, keep all that at bay, but if at any moment I feel you're in danger, you become more important than my entire life.

"When that happens, you will own me."

Whoa. Talk about some serious stuff. "Is that all?" I joked.

He cupped my chin in his hand and tipped my face to his. Axel kissed me long and slow and in that moment I knew the steel-lined connection between us couldn't easily be severed by a word or a callous action. It was deep, it was strong, and most important, it made my toes curl.

"So what does this mean?" I whispered.

"It means I'm sorry and I made a mistake. Next time, I'll tell you everything that's going on. Everything and I won't put distance between us."

I glared at him. "The next time you put distance between us, we're not getting back together."

"Agreed."

Something struck me. "But what about you shifting today? What was that about?"

Axel's jaw clenched and his eyes darkened. "I don't know. I'm not sure if it was because of Adam or what."

I squeezed his hand. "Maybe it was only a fluke. A one-time thing."

"I hope so."

He wrapped an arm around me. "Now, do you want to get out of here?"

"Where are we going? On a real date?"

A flare blazed in his eyes. Axel winked at me. "Yep. In fact, I know a great little place that's only open one more night."

"Let me guess."

Ten minutes later we were seated outside the pop-up barbecue joint enjoying a sandwich and a brew.

I licked a dribble of vinegary sauce from the mound beneath my thumb. "I hope this barbecue place stays here forever. I love having a pit-stop here. I wish they were open all the time."

Axel dabbed his napkin on the side of my mouth. "Me, too. I'm glad I could share it with you."

We spent the next hour laughing, eating and relaying stories of our youth. The bond grew between us and by the time Axel dropped me off at Betty's house, I felt confident that our relationship would only flourish.

"I'll see you tomorrow?" I said.

He shook his head. "I've got some work out of town for a few days. I'll be back by the weekend, though. Maybe we can have a date that doesn't involve anyone getting hurt."

I laughed. "Sounds like a plan."

He kissed me goodbye and I entered the quiet house. Betty sat quietly by the fire reading a book and Amelia and Cordelia must've been up in their rooms.

"You get everything straightened out with that boyfriend of yours?"

I smiled. "In fact, I think I did."

"No shotgun tonight?"

Betty shook her head. "No. I think you've earned the right not to be greeted by it. The girls told me what happened. You're a strong one, Pepper Dunn."

"Thanks, Betty. That means a lot."

I climbed the stairs to my room, exhausted. I slipped under the covers and awoke the next morning. The sun sliced through the curtains and birds chirped outside. It was a glorious day to be alive.

I scampered downstairs with Hugo right on my heels. Betty snapped open *The Cauldron News* local paper. "You made the paper," she said.

I snatched a slice of bacon from a plate and crunched through my sentence. "Yeah, and thanks for not telling me that Axel had a twin. You could've eased a lot of heartache for me."

Betty flattened the paper on the table. "It wasn't my place to tell. If he had wanted you to know, he would've told you. That's how it goes. Besides, it was for your own protection."

Cordelia slathered butter on a biscuit. "So what are you going to do with Hugo? Now that the whole thing is over."

"I don't know. We don't need a giant dragon running around Magnolia Cove."

"He's a pygmy dragon," Betty said. "He won't grow to be as large as a house. He'll only grow to about the size of a couch. Big enough for you to ride."

"But not large enough to keep in the backyard," I mused. "Nothing easy about these decisions."

"I'm sure we could figure something out," Betty said. "After all, I run this town."

I couldn't help but smile. "Yep, I know you're right."

I finished up breakfast and decided it was time to teach Hugo how to walk on a leash. I snapped it on and we strolled down Bubbling Cauldron toward Familiar Place. I waved to my neighbors, making sure to give Carmen a great big smile and also Theresa and Harry, the owners of Castin' Iron, the shop where I'd gotten my riding skillet.

I unlocked the door to my store and felt a deep swell of pride as Hugo waddled in. The animals yawned and fluttered awake. I went about my daily duties until the doorbell tinkled above.

Idie Claire Hawker walked in, all three feet of hair and high heels.

"Morning," I said.

"Morning," she said, her gaze floating about the room. "How've you been?"

"Holding up," I said. "And yourself?"

Idie twisted her fingers. "Well, I wanted to see if you would be interested in something."

I cocked a brow. "What is it? And if you're trying to get me in your chair for a haircut, I know I'm overdue. I'll come in the next month or so."

Idie shook her head. "It's not that. You know I'm a medium, right?'

"You told me."

"I wanted to offer a chance for you to talk with your mother."

I sucked in air. My voice shook. "What?"

"I thought you wanted to know the message she left Mysterio. Together, we can see what it was."

I bit my lip. I wanted to know. All these days that thought had occupied me, wormed its way into the pit of my stomach. It was the one thing I'd been searching for and had eluded me.

"Sure. When do we start?"

So I didn't officially open Familiar Place for about thirty more minutes. Idie and I turned off the lights in the office, lit a couple of candles that she had brought and got started.

I closed my eyes and concentrated, really hoping that the desk between us wasn't going to start bouncing like in some stupid horror flick.

Luckily, it didn't. Instead, a warm feeling of calm crept over me. It was like a thick fog of energy, but it felt soothing, like an incredible blanket of goodness.

"Open your eyes," Idie said.

I blinked. There, standing beside her, was the image of my mother. Her ghostly hair flowed around her face and her dress fluttered as if in some invisible wind. The sweet scent of gardenia blossoms filled the room.

"It was the same smell that filled the night air when you and I sat on the swings," Idie said. "Do you remember? She was with you then."

I nodded. "I do remember."

It had been her favorite scent, as Betty had said.

The ghostly image of my mother floated in the air on an invisible current. Her lips curled into a smile and I felt an overwhelming sense of love and goodness drifting off her.

"She has a message for you," Idie said.

I nearly leaped over the table. "What is it?"

"That she loves you and that you must be strong, for the tide that's about to happen will challenge and scare you. It will make you want to give up this new life. But don't, because there's much goodness in store for you."

I frowned. "She couldn't have told me this at the show?"

Idie shrugged. "I don't judge. I'm only the messenger."

I glanced at the ghostly figure, knowing that more than likely I'd never see her again. "I love you, Mom."

With that, she vanished, but not before she brought her fingers to her mouth and blew me a kiss. A cool wind fluttered through my hair.

I shivered. "Thank you," I said to Idie. "That was the best gift anyone could've ever given me."

"You're welcome," she said kindly. "Now, I'd best be gettin' out of here. I've got some hair to tease. And no, it's not my own."

I righted the room, feeling a huge wave of satisfaction. My skin prickled with energy from the meeting with my mother. Must've been some sort of ethereal after effect or something.

Whatever it was, I had to say it was awesome.

I stretched, feeling as secure as I've ever felt, though the words Idie had spoken drifted like a ghost in my head.

Something trying was coming. An even that would make me want to leave Magnolia Cove and forget about this new life.

I cracked my knuckles. It was time to do some serious magical practice. I'd done some in the past, but really controlling my magic eluded me. Maybe that's where Hugo came in. He was supposed to be the rock that harnessed my power and helped me to become the best head witch ever.

Or so I hoped.

I stretched. Hugo watched me with curiosity. I patted his head and said, "Okay boy, I guess you and I have some training to do."

The door shot open as if a great wind had snapped it to. I jerked, stumbling as a force of magic pushed me back.

The birds squawked. The kittens meowed. The puppies barked.

Standing in the doorway was Rufus Mayes. He wore his usual black leather from head to foot. Black eyeliner rimmed his eyes and the smirk on his face told me he saw victory at hand.

"What are you doing here?" I said, standing. "You're not supposed to enter Magnolia Cove."

"Well, here I am," he said, sauntering in. "And I don't see anyone stopping me."

My heart thundered against my chest. This was bad. This was very bad.

"What do you want?" I said.

Rufus smiled. "Why, you, of course. This time, nothing's going to interfere."

Last time Rufus showed up at Familiar Place, the birds attacked, sending him reeling from the store. I could only hope the same thing would happen again.

Or better yet, that I could use my magic.

I fisted my hands. "And what makes you think nothing's going to stop you?"

Rufus raised a hand. "Because you and I are leaving."

I lunged. Rufus snapped his fingers.

Familiar Place melted away and I was plunged into darkness.

Alone.

With Rufus.

ABOUT THE AUTHOR

Amy Boyles grew up reading Judy Blume and Christopher Pike. Somehow, the combination of coming of age books and teenage murder mysteries made her want to be a writer. After graduating college at DePauw University, she spent some time living in Chicago, Louisville, and New York before settling back in the South. Now, she spends her time chasing two preschoolers while trying to stir up trouble in Silver Springs, Alabama, the fictional town where Dylan Apel and her sisters are trying to master witchcraft, tame their crazy relatives, and juggle their love lives. She loves to hear from readers! You can email her at amy@amyboylesauthor.com.

CPSIA information can be obtained
at www.ICGtesting.com
Printed in the USA
LVHW102138270323
742790LV00014B/175